49

Leonie Stevens was born in Melbourne in 1962, the year that Even Stevens won the Melbourne and Caulfield Cups. Her gambling-mad family won a fortune because she was the fourth child and second girl. Her father comes from staunch Labor True Believer stock and her mother from Dimboola. 'Draw from that what you will,' she says, 'I have over the years, believe me.'

Leonie started writing at eleven, when the first typewriter came into her home. *Nature Strip* is her first novel. She is most comfortable in the margins, and lives with her partner and daughter near Sydney.

Nature
STRIP

LEONIE STEVENS

Wakefield Press

Wakefield Press
Box 2266
Kent Town
South Australia 5071

First published 1994

Edited by Jane Arms
Cover and book designed by design BITE
Typeset by Clinton Ellicott
Printed and bound by Hyde Park Press, Adelaide

Cataloguing-in-publication data

Stevens, Leonie, 1962–
Nature Strip

ISBN 1 86254 308 9

I. Title

A823.3

Publication of this title was assisted by the
Commonwealth Government through the
Australia Council, its arts funding and
advisory body.

To Paul, for the nine-and-a-half years
In memory of Laughing Boy

Contents

'What does not kill me makes me stronger.'
Friedrich Nietzsche

CHAPTER ONE

The bacteria breeder

The pylons rushed past the window like blurred hallucinatory needles, giant grey, collapsing under the purple smog that hovered close to the ground. Steel clouds allowed meagre light to filter in smaller and slower particles. Perhaps an eclipse was on the agenda. Or an apocalypse. I was a microscopic parasite thrusting into a gurgling alien system. But I would be okay. I had my Walkman.

I'm alive/I'm dead/I'm the stranger/killing an Arab –

With a blurt and not much else, the undoubtedly married dough man who'd been trying to crack onto me since Yass Junction rose to his feet and swayed away, the pylons and wreckage of the rail yards flashing by in stereo windows, propelling him to an uncertain home. At the carriage exit door he stopped and endeavoured to deliver some parting gesture – a nod, a slight wave, perhaps – but a baby-carrying woman flung the door open and it hit him across the back of the head, sending a general 'Ooooh' around the carriage, before the commuters turned their attention once more to the bleak landscape.

A jolly voice from a small speaker announced our imminent arrival, as if the carriage captives were eager with anticipation. Well, perhaps the other passengers were eager. The grey reflected in their faces as they peered aimlessly from the windows made me doubt it. Some began to collect their possessions from around their seats. Young children squealed: younger ones bawled.

It's all right, our arrival is imminent. After what seemed like eight years going through the longest, dirtiest rail yards this side of Madras, I reserved the right to be sceptical. Not that I have seen the rail yards in Madras. Or anywhere else, for that matter. But my brother had travelled extensively by train in his youth and seemed to remember every journey. In a squalid third-class carriage in India, he met a man who was to change his life. A holy man. Weaving a fishing net with calloused fingers, he unfolded the secrets of the mystical union for James, who probably droll-eyed lapped it up, shameless hippie that he was, until the next train, and the next holy man. India was full of them, James would tell me. Thank you, I'd reply, I'll know to stay well clear.

Painfully, the train eased alongside a dirty platform. I caught a glimpse of the city from between buildings – a man and a woman in office dress, heads bent down against the wind, grim and determined. A shot-put of nervous disease swept through my vital organs. 'Stop it, Caitlin,' I said out loud. The people queuing up to squeeze out of the carriage door turned to me with blank, suspicious faces. I stared back, more blank and suspicious, and fought off the inclination to explode simultaneously from every orifice.

At crisis point, the dough man made a dazed reappearance and an offer of a lift somewhere, anywhere. He stood over the seat, blocking the exit. I contemplated pulling the emergency cord, but the train was stationary, and the meagre crew were zig-zagging around the platform in case-carrying dodgems. The dough man was big, with a clumsiness suggesting that his commonsense was not in order. His expression said, 'What, a woman on her own who won't accept a lift? She's asking for it.' If I had accepted the lift, I would have been asking for more.

A banging on the window inches away from my head took my attention from the dough man, and the colour drained from his face. I glanced around and saw Roman waving at me. The dough man took one look at him and disappeared. Suddenly, Roman was inside the train and bounding down the empty carriage, yelling, his green eyes luminous, his green hair complementary.

'Your train was late! Jordan's in the cafeteria with a paper bag over her head, and I'm fending off the men in white coats. We got an eviction notice this morning, some Hells Angels have taken over the bottom part of the house, and my dole cheque's late!' He collapsed into the seat opposite me.

'Quiet morning, eh?' I said, rocked out of the tedium by his enthusiasm.

Roman grinned at me, then stood up and made a performance of shaking my hand and telling me how pleased he was that I had ventured out of my cocoon. He was convincing. His father was a big man in the State Sewerage Scene, and had undoubtedly taught him a thing or two.

'I dunno if we'll have a home to go back to,' he confessed after a tussle over who was going to bear the burden of my bag, 'but if we're homeless – then I can really show you around.' Laughing at Roman's flair for the melodramatic, I stepped off the train as a crack of thunder exploded around our ears. The crowds up and down the platform screamed and dived for cover. Roman included. Me, I knew it was just a crack of thunder.

'Hit the train!' voices echoed. 'Lightning hit the train.' The bodies straightened up rather sheepishly. Roman picked up my bag again and giggled as we entered the main concourse of the station.

Hail began pelting on the roof and streets that were barely visible through the bodies huddled against the plate-glass doors. Just like John Brack's painting, I would have thought, had not I been part of some miniature stampede through a peak-hour crowd.

My bag on his back, his arm around my shoulder, Roman raced me through the crowd and up the fake marble steps to the restaurant, stopping squadrons of office workers with his lime-green hair, leather gear and studs. It was quite an honour to walk beside such an exotic creature.

Plumb in the centre of the railway cafeteria, formica tables and vinyl chairs was a tall body in a clown suit with a square paper bag on its head. 'Mr Tuckerbag', it said. No doubting it. She hadn't changed. Success, or the threat of it, wasn't going to inhibit Jordan's mania.

'You made it,' she said when I sat down. 'I knew you weren't a completely slack hippie.' I cringed as Roman dropped my bag heavily on the floor.

'I'm not a hippie. And you've picked up a smart mouth.'

'It's all right,' Roman said, 'being a hippie is nothing to be ashamed of.'

'I'm not a hippie!' I roared, beginning to get irate.

Jordan winked at Roman knowingly. '"Methinks she doth protest too much."'

Shakespeare. It was never too early in the day for Jordan to quote the immortal bard. The very first time we met, five years ago, she was at it.

She'd been a fourteen-year-old huddled in the corner of the Health Food shop at its grand opening. Much to her mother's dismay, she was growling, '"Ye jest at scars that never felt a . . . a . . ."' My friend Dorland and I looked at each other – stage one of the repertoire we'd established to keep us sane in the midst of a peer group of virtual morons.

He giggled. It was a small idiosyncrasy he now allowed himself, being fourteen and a good height and on the post-pubescent side of the sexual expectations he abhorred but nevertheless followed to the letter.

The face beneath the curly grey-blonde hair looked up. Grey-blue eyes taunted *us* as morons. 'Don't tell me,' she said. 'I know this one.'

If she knew it, she didn't reveal herself. Or rather, her mother didn't give her a chance to reveal herself. The photographer from the local newspaper was there, all prepared to document the opening of our town's first health food store, and Kit didn't want her lunatic daughter to make the front page. Jordan was bustled out through bead curtains to the nether regions that lay behind such shops. Dorland and I looked at each other. We'd never been behind a shop before, except when we were seven years old, helping James to care for the newsagent's when Penny Hanson's husband left her and she went into instantaneous labour. The whole town rallied around to help look after the news-agency and her two other children, until it became public that one of these do-gooders had been helping themselves to the till, and to Penny's oldest daughter Joanne, who was seven. Being a small town, gossip was rife, and when John Jackson suddenly packed up his butcher's shop and left town, it was assumed he was the culprit.

Dorland and I had our own ideas. 'So what,' James said with a laugh when we told him, 'you two always have your own ideas.' Then he apologised for his rudeness, and listened to the evidence we had collected about Mr Zeidars, local high school principal and coach of the under-eight's netball team. It was a common thing for him to get the younger high school kids to bare more than their hands for the cane. And when a boy and a girl in my class were caught at it behind the sports shed, he made them perform the act in front of him in his office. The other students were too paralysed by his authority to think of him as any-thing more than a right bastard. But Dorland and I knew more. James listened to us intently, then spoke quietly to a few of the parents. They shook their heads at him, prob-ably thought, Trouble-making hippie. If it was good enough for me, it's good enough for my kids. Which meant they wanted their kids to be humiliated and terrified, just as they had been. They were still scared of Teacher.

And so we published the unofficial newsletter that got Dorland, as the perceived ringleader because of his gender, expelled, and me, as the brainless sheep because of my gender, a two-week suspension.

'Two weeks?' I said. 'Whatever happened to equal pay for equal work?' Zeidars, in the midst of some kind of seizure, immediately sent for James. I suppose he thought James might exact some terrible discipline on me. But James was smashed at the time, and he just nodded at Zeidars and said, 'Yes, yes, I'm thoroughly disgusted!'

As we walked out of the principal's office and down the

corridor, towards the double doors of freedom, we were on top of the world. Dorland and I didn't give a toss about the school. The work held no challenge, the students and teachers no promise. The full implications of Dorland's sentence did not hit us until we stepped out into the glaring sunshine, when we came face to face with his grandmother and guardian, Mrs Stafford, otherwise known as Old Staff. She said two words that took the victorious smiles off our faces.

'Boarding school.' It was the beginning of that end.

Going down the ramp from the cafeteria, we were stopped by a couple of young constables. They were jovial as they jibed Roman about his green hair, and wanted to know who was under the Mr Tuckerbag. Jordan lifted the bag, and they both recoiled a little and said, 'Aren't you that actress . . .'

'Ac-TOR!' Jordan said for the thousandth time.

'Oh,' they said, nodding, and guided us through the crowd, across the street, to the head of the taxi queue, and right into a warm, dry Commodore. A spot on a low-quality soap opera had afforded her more privileges than an Amex card. Now bagless, Jordan laughed and stared out onto the street with that infantile exuberance. No, Jordan hadn't changed. Everything and everyone else may have, but Jordan was still that fourteen-year-old crouched in the corner of the health shop, and later in the batik-laden lounge-room, telling us her life story in fifteen minutes flat amid an array of delicious lies. She told us about her mother, Kit, her father, a successful entrepreneurial doctor, her sister, a talentless art student, her brother, a psychotic punk rocker, the dogs, cats, goldfish; and then she shrieked, '"Wound"! "Wound"! I knew it! I knew I knew it!' Dorland and I knew it was stretching the boundaries of our philosophy to believe that people like Jordan existed outside mental homes and city hairdressing salons, but there she was. Fourteen and already harbouring a deep yearning to be an actor.

At eighteen, she had her first job. Billie Randall, lovable scallywag, on 'S'cool'. She'd been filming for three months, and on the air for half that time, yet her stardom was assured. Tall, uniquely beautiful, she stood out among her juvenile co-stars in a key area. Jordan could act. Or, rather, become the part.

She wasn't into method acting. There was no strategy. She just got in there and did it, with a religious zeal that impressed her co-workers, and made her a mark for overseas talent scouts. Offers had begun to arrive from exotic places via her agent. Well, London, Los Angeles. Places more exotic than Melbourne, Australia, anyway. Jordan was nonplussed. Her burning ambitions were to do Shakespeare and to be in a John Waters film. People scoffed when she said this, but to Jordan the two were identical.

'Drop me off here,' she said to the taxi driver at an

anonymous intersection. 'I have one of those meetings. Americans this time.'

I didn't mind. Seeing Jordan for fifteen minutes at the end of a twenty-three-hour train journey was better than not seeing her at all. She punched my shoulder, then darted from the cab before I could respond. Jordan was too scatty to have a complex relationship with anyone. What united us was where we came from, and the years we'd spent in solitude. Especially the years when Dorland was away at boarding school. We kept each other legally sane and infernally optimistic. As the Mr Tuckerbag went back over her head and she disappeared into the blurred landscape, I knew that even if we never met again, she would be the best friend I would ever have.

The little I could see of the town from the taxi window made me doubt the sanity of Melbourne's town planners. Tiny cottages were squashed along boulevards wide enough to carry whole armies. Even the side lanes were bombastic. I would have asked Roman about it, but he'd fallen asleep by the time we crossed the river. Something about a late, hard night.

When I first set eyes on Roman, two years earlier, he'd had a couple of late, hard nights. Dropping plumb into our little town after twenty-three hours on the train, he came straight to the hospital with Jordan. From the moment he walked into the ward, hair dyed bright orange and T-shirt saying, 'I want to be sick', I wanted to know where people like him congregated, so I could join them.

'This is Roman,' Jordan said. 'He's an old mate of my brother's, but don't hold that against him.'

'Who,' I said, 'your brother?'

Roman pulled a face and said, 'Charming.'

'You think this is charming,' Jordan told him, 'wait till she's recovered.'

'What,' Roman laughed, looking around at my bandages and drips and multi-coloured bruises, 'are you ill?'

I wasn't for long. Not with Roman around. We clicked like a detonator and some friendly dynamite. In truth, his rebellion was all fashion-related. He didn't want to destroy society, or be an anarchist, or play bad guitar. Just to look like he did. And, like he always told his father, the sewerage superintendent, social acceptance is just a bottle of Decore Blue Black away.

When the taxi pulled up at the front of a dilapidated mansion on a beachfront boulevard, Roman took me in his arm and under his wing and into the eye of a culture shock that left me speechless for the best part of thirty seconds. True, some Hells Angels were camped out in the hall and in the front two rooms of the first floor. But they were watching 'Play School', and doing the Wiggly Woo with an excited pair of three year olds. One of them – an enormous fellow named Ivan who looked like one of the rednecks from 'Deliverance' – came over and chatted to Roman, then me, and it turned out that he'd known James quite a long time ago, when James was a tearaway, in and out of trouble in the Kings Cross of the sixties.

'So you're the little sister he took up to the North Coast,' Ivan said with a booming laugh which I interpreted to be irony. 'Tell me, is he still growing those killer Afghan heads?' It seemed that James was something of a living legend for those Afghan Heads: the bikies puffed out from the Wiggly Woo started reminiscing about the strongest dope they'd ever smoked, and we took the opportunity to get up the ricketty staircase before I felt compelled to open my bag and offer them a joint of the very same Afghan heads Ivan mentioned. Well, a strain, anyway.

Up on the first floor, not much seemed to be happening. Roman reckoned no one got out of bed before three in the afternoon, unless they had to put their dole forms in. We put my bag in his room, where he had kindly set up a single bed mattress for me, then ventured into the kitchen.

'You won't like this,' he said before opening the door. Perhaps James was right when he suggested having a tetanus booster. The door slid open, and Roman peered inside then recoiled in horror.

It was clean. Spotless. Shoulders dejected as if it was the end of the world, Roman said, 'I don't believe it! This is someone's idea of a sick joke!'

Roman was slumming it. I observed him through the course of that day, then in an increasingly drunken blur at a pub that night, talking to people who might otherwise be classed as degenerates. Personally, I thought that most of them were slumming it, living in abject poverty and torn clothes as some kind of reaction to their affluent upbringing. While it was obviously fake, it was also a lot of fun. Well, where I came from, watching the mushrooms grow was fun, so this ranked as absolute hilarity.

Noise, yelling, colours, names too numerous to remember, and all the time me struggling to keep a lid on my tongue. Keep your guard up, I had promised myself just before the dough man interrupted my solitude at Yass Junction at two the previous morning: smile on call, scowl on call, be polite, say nothing until you're alone, and then don't utter a sound.

Unfortunately, sharing a room with Roman, who snores when he's had a few drinks, meant I wasn't really alone. So I lay in silence until the middle of the night, when all the noise had died down, except a strange humming sound from the Hells Angels vicinity, then crept out, down the hall, to the kitchen. Flick, and the fluorescent light laid bare the kitchen table, a sea of beer bottles, empty chip packets and full ashtrays. I considered cleaning it up to confuse Roman, but I was too wasted. So I pushed the mess to one side, allowing my elbows to rest on reasonably bare laminex.

Done it. Done it. Arrived. The feeling swept over me like a hot flush. I was suddenly in a town where I only knew one human, and Jordan. There was a shabby pretext of going to university, but that didn't fool James, or me. We both knew I had to get out and start a new life, away from the graveyard of my manic adolescence. When Dorland went away, I could survive, because Jordan was there. Without Jordan, it had been hell. And since the accident –

All receptors shut down as my mind forcibly jumped track. I had five hundred dollars in my bank account. Enough to rent a flat somewhere. I'd seen enough in one day to know I couldn't survive sharing a house.

The wall swung in at the door, and Jordan was standing there. Jordan or not Jordan. The face and colouring and stature were the same. Yet this Jordan had black rings under the eyes, and what looked like a three day growth. But it was Jordan. Identical.

'Hhmm!' came a deep, contemptuous sigh. 'You must be the hippie.'

I must have sat there, gawking like a lunatic, long after I realised this was Jordan's brother Shane. The likeness was astounding. The pale skin, blond-grey hair, thin lips – only these were turning into a scowl. The eyes were regarding me with increasing disdain.

'Sorry,' I stammered finally, although I still wasn't really ready to speak, 'it's just – you look so much like Jordan. It's uncanny. You could be twins.'

The eyes rolled and the lips curled, and he walked across the room and put a tray of dishes on the sink. 'How funny you should say that,' he said sarcastically, 'we are.'

Leaving home had been a shock. The train ride had been a shock. Roman and his house and the night out had been a shock. But this was like a full electrocution. It was useless to try and figure out why Jordan had omitted to tell me she had a twin brother. Useless. But the evidence was staring me in the face. Or rather, had its back turned, washing dishes.

In an attempt to salvage some kind of self-respect, I made an offhand comment about him being the phantom dish washer and kitchen cleaner. He pretended not to hear. I figured what Jordan had said all those years ago was true. Her brother had behavioural problems much more serious than hers. And it wasn't just that he washed dishes, either.

'Well,' I said as I began my exit, 'I can't say it's been a pleasure to meet you.'

'I'd be disappointed if it was,' he said, without taking his eyes off the cup he was scrubbing with a steel scourer. I was tempted to tell him he'd scratch off the nice rose print if he kept that up, until I realised it was probably what he was trying to do. Perhaps I would ask Roman what his problem was. Then again, perhaps not. I didn't want to get too involved. No, I concluded, as I crept back into the single bed, after holding Roman's nose so he'd stop snoring and pushing him onto his side, I will rent a little flat and watch from a safe distance. Watch them like a colony of bacteria, multiplying, dividing, dying off. The whole planet was one big bacteria breeder, in a shoddy corner of a train station somewhere. And I was an inconsequential bean.

CHAPTER TWO

The Adonis
and the Iceman

The bathroom was a matchbox harbouring an apologetic midget bath in which a shower hose drooped with no visible means of support; a toilet jammed against the bath so that even I with my short legs had trouble getting in; a cracked pink porcelain hand basin; and above this a mould-ridden medicine chest. Not the kind of place you'd want to keep medicine. And of course, being Melbourne in winter, the entire matchbox was covered with hanging, dripping clothes. The laundrette was four blocks away, and four blocks was too far in the cold and the rain.

I was methodically rinsing out some white socks, thinking, Is this all there is? Life was boring now that Roman had left town. No more parties. No more excuses to get out of doing uni work. Just rinsing out white socks on a Monday night, between bursts of television and essay revision.

'I feel so terrible about this,' Roman had said to me on the very same platform where he met me four months earlier.

Meaning that he had accepted an offer from a family friend to run an imported record business in Sydney. He may have felt terrible, but he didn't look it. A bottle of blue black hair dye had given him a dashingly handsome air. He kissed each of the army of people who had come to see him off, and turned to me at the end and said, 'After I got you to come down here and all . . .'

The porters were yelling and tossing cases onto the train carelessly, and a strong autumn wind was ruining more than a few extravagant hair styles. As Roman's well-wishers ducked for the cover of the terminal, I made it clear that I came down of my own accord. I had a course of study to undertake, remember? He laughed at me, because he knew full well that my attendance wasn't what it should be. I knew full well it would improve once he left town.

As the train slid down the platform, I walked through the gate to avoid running into Roman's friends in the concourse. They were nice enough people, most of them, and would probably suggest I join them to get good and drunk. The chances were, if I did, I would open my mouth and not be able to close it. Anyway, they were Roman's friends, not mine. So I walked on the footpath beside the building, dodged some cars and jumped into a waiting tram. It slid off up the hill, carrying me back into anonymity, into the belly of a large and heavily polluted beast. No, I didn't mind being alone. It was my natural habitat.

Two days later, Jordan had called from Tennant Creek,

or somewhere equally ridiculous. America had beckoned with a suitable offer – a small part in a David Lynch film – and she was unstoppable. Jordan's absence wasn't such a big deal, because even in presence she was often absent, pupils fully dilated as she directed her hallucinations of the perfect Lady Macbeth. She stayed at my flat for a couple of weeks when she was fired from 'S'cool', and the media were staking out her flat. I learnt one important thing about her in that short time: I would never, ever, live with her. She melted all of my saucepans, broke all the glasses and most of the plates, and caused stains on just about every square foot of carpet and wall. The material world was a blur to her, and her motor skills were somewhat retarded, so I took to hiding my breakables and spreading plastic on the floor and furniture.

'You'd get on well with my father,' she told me. 'He's got covers on everything. Even a cake-keeper over the telephone. And I won't even tell you what Shane does.'

No, I thought, please don't.

She flew out to Hollywood from Sydney airport, so I didn't get a chance to say goodbye.

When I first started talking to myself, I was concerned. I contemplated getting a cat, but decided that would inject pathos into what was a fact of life. It wasn't as if I didn't have anyone to talk to. There were people at uni, and the man at the local milk bar, and Roman on the phone, and the odd new acquaintance, although there hadn't been many of them for weeks. Not since the disaster with the Adonis of the photocopying machine.

He was eye-catching, no doubt about it. Erect black mohawk, leather pants and jacket with slogans written across the back. Pierced ears and nose, and Doc Marten boots. Normally I wasn't prone to having my attention taken by men, but this one was exotic for sure, and my time with Roman had given me a taste for it. I fumbled through semiotics notes, doing my best not to stare, but finally I was caught red-eyed and shameless.

'Hello there,' his voice said brightly, and it took me a moment to realise he was talking to me. He was like a punk from a TV commercial – incredibly good looking, fresh, clean skin, a nice kid from a good home in fancy dress. 'You're a friend of Roman's, aren't you?'

Sublime luck. Of the thousands of people in this city, we had a common denominator. I nodded as I gave the impression of sorting through my photocopying.

'Thought so,' he continued, ceasing his business to lean on the machine. 'My memory's not so good – all the alcohol, probably – but I remember you. You were unconscious on Roman's bed. He was telling me, "Oh, you have to meet this girl, she's just like Jordan, only more clever," but there you were, paralytic, and I said I thought you were more like Shane.'

I glared at him playfully. 'Thanks a lot.' He was grinning. I stepped forward and thrust out my hand, saying, 'Caitlin Steele.'

He shook my hand. 'Brendan Kennelly.' I almost replied, Would you like to go to bed with me? such was the immense beauty of this boy, but I restrained myself and went back to my copying.

He told me he'd been on a brilliant acid trip last night until someone – he suspected himself – suggested having a seance. It all got out of control: Shane's girlfriend went into convulsions, and Brendan's cat ran away.

I had to stifle a laugh. 'Is she all right?'

'No, I can't find her, that's why I'm copying up these notices.'

'No, numbskull,' I said, shaking my head and giggling, 'Shane's girlfriend.'

He grinned. 'Oh, Lisa's all right. As all right as Lisa ever is.' As an afterthought, he said, 'I was a St John's Ambulance boy. I know CPR and all that stuff.'

'Oh, really?' I said. 'Perhaps you can give me a lesson.' I helped him stick up his lost cat notices, and he helped me carry home a desk that I'd been unable to move from a second hand shop. We smoked some dope, watched Jordan on repeats of 'S'cool', talked about Roman a little, then went out that night to hear some live music at a once-glorious but now extremely suspicious establishment in St Kilda. Brendan seemed to know every single person there, and he must have introduced me to all of them. After a couple of hours, my head was swimming with names and alcohol. I thought my luck was really in: Brendan was as charming as he was good looking. Something I should have figured, though: men like him are rarely ever single.

Brendan's face shot pale as we hovered at the bar, and I turned in time to see Deidre coming through the glass doors and towards us at an alarming pace and with an alarming demeanour. Dressed in Bride of Frankenstein mode, she was probably the schoolyard bully. I doubted that she would listen to reason, or even understand a word of more than two syllables, so I made a run for it. Zipped past her, out the doors and down the steps. I fell on the last one and twisted my ankle, but even this wasn't enough to stop me running across the road to a waiting taxi. I didn't feel safe until I was in my flat with the door locked and bolted twice. The following day, I dyed my hair black and took to wearing sunglasses. I noticed Brendan in the street a few times, as he lived in my area, and I hid in laneways or behind trees, much to the amusement of the kids from the local primary school, who seemed to catch me at it every time. They thought I was putting on a show for them. I decided it was better to keep right away from people than to risk a repeat performance.

My knuckles were as white as the socks before I realised I'd been wringing the water and the life out of them for several minutes. I placed them over the towel rail, knowing it would take at least a week for them to dry. Nevertheless, I felt a certain satisfaction that I was looking after myself. If doomsday came tomorrow, at least I would fry up in clean socks.

It was the first day of spring. The newsreader had just said so, before adding that it was going to be the coldest night so far this year. Two degree minimum. Then they ran a Greenhouse effect story. Greenhouse was not yet a household word, and the cable news report was making out that two scientists being interviewed were mad. Global warming? The yuppie in Armani smiled and said, 'Time will tell.'

A soft tap on my door. It startled me for a moment, until I realised it was probably someone at the wrong flat. I never had visitors.

It was Shane Brophy. Or else, Jordan on a surprise visit doing a very good impersonation of a male junkie. I was tempted to scream, for I seriously doubted someone like him would be on my doorstep unless he aimed to rob or kill me. Once we had spoken, just once, on the night I arrived, in the kitchen. We'd crossed paths many times since, as for some inexplicable reason Roman counted him as his best friend, but we generally just pulled faces at each other and thought dire thoughts. Perhaps it was a mirage: a cathode ray-induced hallucination. I asked, 'Are you corporeal?'

Running a hand through his short hair wet with rain, he said, 'Reportedly.' He was really awkward, and so was I, for that matter, because I still couldn't look at him without seeing Jordan, and I didn't know what the hell he was doing there.

'Do you want to come in?' I said, because the weather outside was really foul, and the flat was losing its cosiness. I hoped to the God whose existence I vehemently denied to the feminist discussion group that he would say no: that he had a message from Roman, or that he was lost. It seemed to take him a long time to make up his mind. Probably because, as I'd always suspected, he was unbelievably stupid. Finally he shuffled inside, and we stood there in the lounge-room for a few agonising moments, because I couldn't figure out why he was there, and he seemed unable to speak. Finally, he sighed and folded his arms.

'Would you believe I dreamt that I had to come and see you before I go to Sydney?'

I shrugged, now completely mystified. For him to be there at all was a turn up: his attempt at friendliness blew away all my preconceptions.

'I suppose so,' I said, 'I had a dream once that I was Nancy Reagan, and that I really loved Ronnie.' He almost cracked a smile. I was amazed that it was possible. I'd never seen his mouth curving upwards: it was usually as if he'd had a stroke. There was a long, tortuous silence, and I couldn't decide whether he was stupid, arrogant or extremely shy.

'Sydney, hey? First Roman, now you. What's the great

attraction, anyway? No, don't tell me, it's probably illegal and against one of the commandments.' I paused, then folded my arms to match his. 'Your turn.'

He asked if I wanted to go and see 'Eraserhead' with him. I thought I was hearing things: this was more ludicrous than the plotline of 'Dynasty', which had just come on TV. In a clearer mind I would have laughed and shown him the door but, alas, I'd been talking to myself more than I cared to and, although this guy appeared to be on an isolated farm with the lines down, he was better than 'Dynasty'. Anything was better than 'Dynasty'. We were both surprised when I said yes.

He had a beaten up old Renault, and he was a terrible driver, especially in the appalling weather conditions. Somehow we made it to Victoria Street, then down through Little Saigon to the Valhalla. On that night, it was Valhalla: dry, warm and peopled. The hum of conversation floating through the air compensated for our not really talking: we didn't actually have anything to say. I made out that I was highly interested in the film calender, and he kept his eyes on the carpet. Then we queued up and went inside.

The film itself was an intense experience, like a protracted, bad dream. I was transfixed by horror: I didn't understand any of it. Now, I considered myself something of an amateur film buff, and my complete lack of comprehension was a severe blow to my ego. Which ego? Christ, out with a guy like Shane Brophy, ego barely mattered any more. Despite this, or perhaps because of it, it was the most remarkable film experience I had ever undergone. Especially when the power failed towards the end of the film, and the theatre was plunged into pitch darkness.

In the blackness there was uproar, as if people thought calling out 'Where's the lights?' was going to bring the power back on. One person started screaming, and then another, and suddenly people were scrambling to try and find their way out, which was ludicrous, not to mention dangerous, in the circumstances.

'Man,' I said, more to myself than anyone else, 'people are so uncool.'

'Nobody says "man" any more,' Shane said from somewhere on my left. 'Fossilised hippie colloquialisms.'

'Oh, excuse me, Mr Angry Young Man, I suppose the only reason you're talking to me in public is because it's pitch black and no one can see you! You're so cool! If I wasn't vegetarian, I'd stick you in a box and fill it up with offals and livers and blood sausage!' I chuckled to myself at my own wit, which was pathetic when you come to think about it.

'I didn't know you were a vegetarian,' he replied in a milder and more surprised tone.

'Of course I am!' I almost shrieked. 'I'm a bloody hippie!'

I wasn't a hippie. I wasn't aligned to any subcultural formation. Hell, I hadn't known what I was since the age of six. Before that, I knew I was bored. Bored stupid. I was walking through life like Robert Mitchum, half asleep. That was before Dorland. When he moved in with Old Staff at the neighbouring property, Shady Rest, all life began. Dorland was clever and funny and knowledgeable. He had travelled the world three times with his mother, who gave him up for a French fashion designer who hated kids. The bright bespectacled eyes had seen things I hadn't dreamed of. Six-year-old Caitlin got caught, spun around, spun out. She didn't know whether she wanted to be Dorland, or later Jordan, or James, or just sleepy old Robert Mitchum again. Twenty-year-old Caitlin knew one thing. She wasn't going to be patronised by an arrogant arsehole who was only talking to her because of a dream.

'So what's your REAL motive, frosty boy? Why are you sitting in a theatre with a social *faux pas* like me?'

'I don't know, but I think I'll seek therapy.'

'That's probably a very good idea.'

'That's probably why I'll never do it.'

All of a sudden, every light in the whole theatre came on full blast, including the projector, which was now showing a Bugs Bunny cartoon – unless it was part of 'Eraserhead'. Shane's skin was deathly pale under the bright lights, the dark rings under his eyes almost purple, the eyes themselves bloodshot and nervous. I realised two things. One, he was nothing like Jordan. And two, in his angry young man act, he was a lousy performer. Both of these realisations intrigued me.

In the foyer with a theatre-load of people similarly displaced by the film and the blackout experience, all I could say was, 'What a far out trip!' I grinned at him expectantly, letting him know I'd caught a glimpse past his cool facade. He gave the smile a shadow of a chance.

'I found it quite . . . purging.'

'Purging?' I roared. 'Who needs purging? You can buy little chocolate tablets for purging!'

'Do you have to shout?' he said.

'Incessantly. Genetic predisposition.'

He clapped his hands. 'Big word, Caitlin, well done.'

I pulled a face. 'Try this then. I – think – I – need – a – drink.'

'You only THINK? I know I need one.'

So we got into the Renault and drove to a pub in Fitzroy that had an open fire blazing and perfect Jamaican coffees. Till closing time we attempted a Freudian analysis of 'Eraserhead'. It was rather futile, especially by the third double Jamaican coffee, when all we could do was argue. We would argue when we agreed, just for the sake of it, because this was a lot easier than communicating as adults. By the fourth double Jamaican coffee, there was no possibility of communicating as adults anyway.

When the pub closed, he offered to drive me home, but I'd been unsure enough of his driving earlier on: now he'd consumed alcohol, I was convinced. On the pretext of showing him some kind of magic trick, I convinced him to hand over his car keys. I promptly handed them to the barmaid, saying he would pick them up in the morning. She complimented me on being a good friend.

Shane exploded in my ears, as we wandered the narrow back streets in search of a taxi. 'You idiot!' he lamented. 'You brainless hippie! You gave away my car keys! She's probably got ten brothers who run a stolen car racket.'

He was so serious all the time that the slightest note of humour in his voice was enough to crack me up. 'Who'd want to steal that bomb?' I roared.

He huffed his shoulders up indignantly and had to work really hard not to laugh himself. 'You're a pain in the arse, Caitlin.'

'No, that's just your anal retentiveness.'

It was still pouring with dirty rain and, as we walked to Brunswick Street to try and get a taxi, he complained all the way that we'd both get pneumonia, and it would be my fault, and I told him that I had a responsibility to Jordan, and if he got pneumonia, it would be because he'd neglected his immune system. We argued for about half an hour, until a taxi happened by.

'Right,' I said brightly, 'who gets dropped off first?'

'You do,' he snarled. 'Preferably from a great height, onto your head.'

I clapped my hands. 'Seven out of ten, Brophy!'

He scowled and said, 'Oh, get lost!'

I opened the taxi door and said, 'You're a masochist:

you'll be back,' and shut the door before he had time to respond. As the car pulled away, leaving him on the saturated sidewalk, I couldn't decide whether he was smiling or grimacing. In the end, taking all things into consideration, I decided it must be wind.

CHAPTER THREE

Making the Adonis
(Six months later)

Every Saturday morning, at nine on the dot, there would be a knock on the door. It was the landlady, an elderly Greek woman, who spoke no English, and her pretty young daughter, the latter's palm open to receive the rent money. I would watch them from my front window, in a futile attempt to see something of interest, something to give them a stronger identity than just 'The Land-lords'. Alas, the most I ever saw was the old lady scratch her bum.

Kyle would pay them, then usually come into my room and tell me about the previous night. Who said what to whom, who did what to whom, what everyone else had to say about it and, invariably, who she'd spent the night with. No matter how good her casual partner had been, she always slipped out at dawn to come home, on the pretext of paying the rent. Actually, she just didn't like facing her conquests in the cold light of morning. It was one thing to get drunk, go home with someone and fuck like crazy: it was another to have them make coffee for you. I usually said to her, 'I should be so lucky', and she usually said, 'You should be'.

Some time after that, we would walk down the hall-way, past Kyle's door, through the lounge-room which was always a disaster area and probably a potential health hazard, to the kitchen. On Saturday mornings, there were usually bottles on the tables and benches, and all the cups and glasses and even jars would have frothy beer residue around them. We would drink coffee, gossip, then go for a stroll down Brunswick Street to check out the op shops before any of the other fashion hounds did. After a visit to our favourite café, where we indulged in more coffee and gossip, we would wander home with our bags full of junk and clothes we would probably never wear.

By then it would be lunch-time. Dominic would have cleaned up the kitchen and be sitting there reading the newspaper. All the political and human interest stories. When he heard us coming, he would quickly turn to the comics, and put on one of his Nazi-punk tapes. Dominic was very image conscious: he didn't want to give the impression of having anything between his ears apart from the metal plate he acquired in a car accident several years earlier. He was proud to be a Nazi Punk.

'Yo,' Kyle would say. 'Hey, brother,' I would say. Dominic hated anything even vaguely American, so he would scowl at us, and make a big deal of folding up the newspaper, as if we had spoiled his scrutiny of the comics, and he would tell us about the havoc he and his mate Mad Lenny had caused the previous night.

Usually in the midst of Dominic's Mad Lenny stories, Brendan would come down. He would flip out Dominic's Oi music and put on some tuneless American thrash. He would beam at us, ask to see what we'd got on our shopping blitz, then admonish us for our kitsch taste. If he wasn't so intent on being macho, Brendan would have really enjoyed collecting bits and pieces. But, as it was, his room was bare, apart from the necessary furniture, Black Flag posters on the walls and his immense record collection.

Within two minutes, and half a dozen thrash songs, Dominic would have tried to put his tape back on, and the two of them would argue, and I would distract them by jumping on the sink, or something, while Kyle got one of her Cure tapes and put that on. Both the boys would yell, 'No, No!' and we would say that we had the numbers and were exercising our democratic privilege.

'What about Marcie?' Dominic would say. 'What about her?' we would reply. Right on call, Marcie would stumble into the kitchen, still off her face from the pills she took two days ago. 'Wanna hear a tape?' we'd ask. Kyle would say, 'What tape?' Marcie usually just went, 'Ugh', which was close enough to 'Cure' to win the argument for us. In this manner, five of us in the kitchen – well, four, Marcie didn't really count – we would launch into another day. Discuss the options for the night. Who was having a party, whose band was playing where and, when Marcie left the room, how long we were going to keep covering her rent. In the end we always decided, a bit longer. It had been like that for six months, since I moved in.

The household hadn't always been so congenial. When I first went to see the room in response to an eviction notice and an advertisement in a bookshop window, Kyle met me at the door with a glum expression that said, You're not going to like this. It was early spring, extremely cold, and the house was like a morgue.

The front room, which was vacant, was as big as the entire flat I was moving out of. It had polished wood floor-boards, a long-disused open fireplace, and the high ceiling appeared to be shrouded by mist. Along the hallway were boxes and bags and empty pizza packets that looked to be seventies vintage. Three complete three-piece suites were piled on top of one another in the lounge-room. The kitchen was a complete shambles, as the pressure cooker had exploded a week ago, and there was an argument over who was supposed to clean it up. Worst of all, the bathroom was outside, and the toilet door had fallen off.

Kyle had said very little to me as she showed me around, and I thought I understood why. But when she made me a cup of coffee and started to talk, the picture became more interesting. There were four of them living there at the moment: two of them had been a couple, until recently, and the atmosphere between them was dreadful. The other guy had just broken up with his girlfriend, and she kept coming around, trying to commit suicide in front of him. Not enough to complete the job, but enough to cause quite a mess and make everyone feel like finishing it for her. And as for herself – Kyle had just realised she was late for her period, and she was going to have to have another abortion.

I didn't know whether to comfort her or run. As it was, I still had half a cup of coffee left, so I decided to drink in the atmosphere, which was thicker than the caffeine. I had almost had my fill when I heard the front door open then slam shut, and heavy footsteps come down the loose floor-boards in the hallway. Kyle immediately rose from her seat and disappeared, and I heard her whispering to someone in the next room that a girl was here to see about the room. Then, Brendan the punk Adonis walked in.

I choked on my last mouthful of coffee. When I regained my breath, I said, 'Forget it, I'm leaving.' The spectre of Deidre was as tangible as he was, standing behind him, the Bride of Frankenstein. Brendan forcibly stopped me while Kyle, completely in the dark about why we were having a virtual tussle in the kitchen, said, 'Looks like you know each other, then.'

The fact was that we were both profoundly embarrassed about what happened with his jealous girlfriend and that he had omitted to tell me about her. I planned to walk out and never set foot within ten blocks of this house again, until he said, 'I'm sorry, I've broken up with her. She's gone to Adelaide!'

'Deidre has?' Kyle said sharply, forgetting about the tussle, 'When? Why wasn't I told?' She was furious that something so major and so inane had slipped past her network, and she implored Brendan to give her all the details.

I said, 'Yes, Brendan, all the details,' not because I really wanted to know, but to make him squirm the way I had that night.

He recounted the events of the previous night with scant elaboration, while Kyle made coffee between constant interjections and demands for detail – 'She WHAT?' – 'But what about all her stuff?' – 'How are Todd and Maxie going to pay the rent?' – 'Did she take my hair dryer with her?'

Brendan glared and almost yelled, 'Screw your hair dryer!' then turned to me and smiled cheerfully. 'So when are you moving in?'

I glanced from him to Kyle several times, and it was decided.

The two of them were my main reasons for opting into the household. When I met Dominic, I was mildly interested but not much more. When I met Marcie, I thought she might be good for a laugh. That was when she had a quick, Benny Hill style sense of humour and before she took to numbing her brain completely at every opportunity. Marcie and Dominic were secondary, though. Kyle reminded me very much of a female version of Roman, and Brendan was just Brendan, impossibly good looking and now, thankfully, available.

Somehow, my presence in the house lifted them all out of the doldrums that came more from lack of purpose than from their unemployment benefits. I went with Kyle to the production-line abortion clinic, where she gossiped with the nurses and returned from the procedure beaming with happiness, the only dark spot that she must refrain from sex for six weeks. I drank beer with Brendan, who was as good natured as he was easy on the eye. He became a vegetarian almost instantly, a highly political one at that, and took to Animal Liberation activism and food without MSG. Deidre was never mentioned. Out came his beaten-up electric guitar. He and Dominic recruited a couple of old mates from the eastern suburbs, and the four of them cleared out all the three-piece suites from the lounge-room and started creating an unholy ruckus at all hours of the day and night.

The neighbours on one side complained profusely but had some sort of philosophical objection to calling the police, so they weren't a problem. On the other side was a household whose levels of depravity rivalled ours: two working girls, who were rather conservative, and two raging queens named Sly and Stuart, who visited our place so often that we ended up tearing down some fence palings to facilitate easy access.

Sly was my favourite, a recent refugee from a highly

conservative middle-class home. He took particular delight in everything, from doing his own shopping to climbing the drain pipes when drunk to see if they were safe enough to climb when he was sober. Together we established a map of all the gay bars, worked out which were free on which nights, which had cheap drinks at which times, then we went on expeditions. Invariably Sly would pick someone up, or usually have his choice of men who wanted to pick him up, such was his exotic appearance. Tall, Eurasian, well spoken and always meticulously dressed in his own wild screen-printed creations, there was no-one like him in the whole club circuit. I always came home alone, but that didn't bother me greatly, because I knew Kyle or Brendan would be up, watching television or listening to music. With the sudden influx of people and experiences, the last thing I needed was to be blinkered, as Kyle put it, by some kind of relationship. And I was too nervous to attempt a one-night stand.

The rare times when I did lie awake in bed at night, feeling empty and in off-hand need of companionship, I thought about love, and that was enough to turn me to stone. I'd seen the face of love, once.

Dorland brought him home for the weekend. His name was Cal. Jordan and I gasped in unison, for we both saw it immediately. The face of a Botticelli angel, soft, perfect, porcelain: a quick, nervous smile and an impossibly soft voice that was infuriating and irresistible. Cal didn't talk much and, when he did, it was so way-out cryptic that we just nodded our heads and said, 'Yeah, Cal.' There was something about him: something close to godliness. What he said always seemed profound. And his packaging was so attractive. I fell in love with him immediately, that first weekend.

The weekends became the highlight of an increasingly mundane existence. Year 11 at high school, and the work still wasn't getting interesting. The weekends were. The two of them would train it up from Sydney and stay at Shady Rest. For a few months, thanks to Cal, we basked in an Indian summer childhood. All I really knew about him was that his father was a diplomat, stationed in the Middle East, and Cal hadn't seen him for more than two years, apart from in dreams, he said. Sitting on the verandah at Shady Rest, Jordan reading Macbeth aloud, Dorland reading *Das Kapital*, Cal shaping and re-shaping the small piece of clay he always carried around, and me not really doing anything at all. And then the Indian summer came to an end. In November.

The four of us decided we needed an independent income. So Jordan and I raided our respective guardians' stashes for marijuana seeds, and we planted a crop in the national park adjoining Shady Rest. A stack of rickety chicken wire was the extent of our agricultural planning. I remember Dorland's face at the time, as he calculated what we would get from the projected crop yield. There was a cold glint in his eyes that was almost thrilling. He put down *Das Kapital* and picked up the *Financial Review*.

Then, he stopped coming up at the weekends. No Dorland meant no Cal. I felt like a vital organ had been wrenched from my body. When the school year finished, Jordan shot straight down to Melbourne to stay with her brother and sister, and maybe get some acting work, something, anything. The solitude became almost unbearable. I concentrated on the dope plants.

Like Santa bearing a great gift, Dorland arrived on Christmas eve, with Cal. At first I was ecstatic. With Jordan gone I had no other friends. No contacts at all, besides James and his friends. But it became obvious from the outset that Dorland didn't want to be there: he'd come to keep Old Staff happy. Dorland was bored. Really bored. Bored with Old Staff, bored with the valley, bored with me. For the first time since the age of six, I faced the concept of a future alone.

It was a long, protracted week. Dorland spent most of it on the telephone and in secret talks with Old Staff, leaving me and Cal together, alone for the most part. This did nothing for my hopeless case of infatuation. It was impossible to tell whether he was highly intelligent or a complete airhead. With Cal, it was all quiet and gentle. No great drama. No great conundrum. Cal just went with the flow.

On New Year's Eve, Cal appeared out of the bush. James

was hosting a party for a hundred or so of his closest friends: Cal looked displaced for a moment, then called me aside. Dorland had split. Just split. Old Staff was being really secretive, but she did say Cal could stay on for the summer if he wanted, so he figured she must feel guilty about something. I just shrugged, as the whole week seemed to be leading to something like this. I followed it to its logical conclusion.

Folding my arms, I snapped at him, 'Pity, there's not a train to take you out of here till tomorrow night.' I remember the look on his face. As if his whole world was falling apart. It really got to me. He had nowhere to go, no one waiting for him. It was a middle-class dilemma. If he was a bit older, he could go searching for the great Australian dream. But he had just turned seventeen, and he didn't want to leave the womb of the valley, the most beautiful place he'd ever known. And he didn't want to leave me, either. It was a pretty speech. I believed it.

The festive season would have been intolerable, with its overt messages of love and love-expression, if I hadn't been living with a bunch of like-minded cynics. We berated the consumerism to camouflage the gnawing kind of loss we all felt. Brendan likened it to finding out there was no Santa. Santa had never been anything but a myth to me, but I knew where Brendan was coming from. It was the loss of childhood. The loss of family. We all knew we weren't going to wake up on Christmas morning and find tinsel and pretty lights and the security of a nuclear family. All single adults, we became an anti-nuclear family. No head, just different corners.

Christmas day, and my flatmates were all heading off to their respective family homes: apart from Marcie, who had trained it to Warrnambool a week early, probably to raid her mother's Valium supply. Kyle and Brendan and even Dominic all took some weird kind of pity on me, as if I was missing out on something. Not having ever been part of a nuclear family, if I was missing something I was blissfully unaware of it, and I was more excitedly looking forward to having the house to myself for a few hours.

They all set off together in the early morning, Brendan planting a piteous kiss on my cheek, when in truth I pitied him, after some of the things he had told me about his family. Parents who fought every Christmas; brother who got smashed and usually vomited on his presents; sister who always expected more, and sulked in her room if she felt she hadn't got the proper allotment. Kyle's family sounded a lot more laid back, because her parents were both agnostic ex-hippie teachers, and they'd given her the money to score some weed to have after dinner. Dominic's family, by his descriptions, usually sat around like lead balloons until the meal was over, then retired to separate parts of the house to sleep it off.

I ate Soyaloaf sandwiches with Sly from next door and

Ben, the boy he'd picked up the previous night. A close friend of Ben was a certain well-known racing car driver, who was sponsored by both a chocolate manufacturer and a champagne importer. So Ben chuffed off and came back after lunch with three boxes of chocolate bars and a case of champagne. His friend the racing car driver was in a generous mood. We sat on Sly's front steps and gave chocolate bars and plastic glasses of champagne to passers by, and talked mainly about men. I lamented the lack of suitable specimens, while Sly and Ben played mock violins.

And then Brendan came home from his suburban tour of duty. We huddled back in the doorway and had to cover Ben's mouth when he tried to wolf whistle, blurting, 'What a butt!' After deciding that Brendan was definitely a suitable specimen, they gave me all kinds of advice on how to *make* him. A few more drinks, and I was game.

I walked up the stairs, along the hall and bashed on Brendan's door. After half-an-hour laying plans, I had no idea of what I was doing. He yelled out, 'Come in.' My hand was on the door handle. I was looking at it. Then I thought of love, and my vision started to swirl. I went to the bathroom and threw up.

CHAPTER FOUR

Desperate living

The summer of 1983 was disgusting. Hot and dirty and miserable. Pollution warnings were issued to asthmatics on the nightly news. A huge drought had hit Victoria, and the water was rationed. That meant that everyone was hot, dirty and reluctant to wash. Not the optimum atmosphere for co-habitation. I spent most of my time hiding out in a back room at the Standard Hotel in Fitzroy. It was the closest point to the air-conditioning duct. The view from the dirty window wasn't very interesting, but I watched it for endless hours, while Brendan and Kyle and a horde of others compensated themselves for the heat with manufactured coolness. Smack. Not that I minded the drug – I had pethidine in hospital once and, despite the circumstances, it made for a jolly time – or even that my friends were using it. They were adults: it was their business. And they kept it their business, which was my only grumble. They never let me in on anything. In their fantasy, I was some kind of innocent. Brendan would peer at me through pin-point eyes, chestnut brown, slits through lazy lids, his slack voice saying, 'It's great that you don't take smack'. It could be forty-five in the shade, and Brendan would be cool. For a while. In the end, he had to surrender to the heat like the bitumen and me, melting and getting warped around the edges.

I always cursed vehemently anyone with the audacity to ring that doorbell before the reasonable hour of midday. Anyone who has lived in a house closely resembling a bus shelter would sympathise: that unmistakable sound haunts you for years afterwards, shooting cold spears of dread down your spine and you think, Here we go again, another day of people bringing around six packs and vomiting outside your window. Of course, if you answer the door to a fond friend, all ill thoughts are shelved and you think, I wonder if they've bought any smoko? and they say, 'Have you got a cigarette?' because they're hanging out too.

On this particular day, though, I was expecting the caller to be Duane, Kyle's yobbo brother and a centre of pestilence. He hung around well after he was asked to leave, and had even started bringing his redneck mates around to get drunk in the lounge-room. Then, one night, he pushed Sly from next door down the stairs when Dominic happened to be around.

Now, Sly wasn't exactly to Dominic's Nazi punk taste. Sly was artistic, Asian, and gay. But he was our next door neighbour, and Dominic was spoiling for a fight. So he taught Duane what that strange phenomenon, punk com-radeship, is all about. As Duane whimpered away, he said he'd be back with his mates to get us all. Poor Kyle was very embarrassed.

I opened the front door with obscenities poised to fly from my tongue, like a furious Jehovah about to spit the pip, but they just dissolved on the spot, because it wasn't Duane at the door. It was Shane Brophy. I stared at him disbelievingly, and he looked equally as shocked to see me. I couldn't get over the change in him. He'd gone to Sydney twelve months ago, a skinny, pale, lethargic kid. What stood in the doorway was a skinny, pale, lethargic man. A strange-looking man at that. Dark eyes set wide apart, dark eyebrows extending almost to the ears. Thin nose, high cheekbones and high, curved forehead. Why hadn't I noticed his forehead before? Damned if I didn't find my-self thinking that he was a most appealing specimen.

'What are you doing here?' he intoned, deadpan, his lips barely moving, but eyes looking as if I was the last person in the world he expected or wanted to see.

'I could ask you the same question, brother,' I replied with the playfulness of one in a superior position, because I knew that I lived there, and he obviously didn't, 'but I doubt you're the type who gives that sort of thing much consideration. Me, I'm here as a joint result of accident of birth and careful deliberation. Most people would doubt that the two concepts – coincidence and cause and effect –

can co-exist. Personally, I find ambiguity the only satisfactory explanation for the human condition.'

Even he could not disguise his confusion. Perplexed eyes squinting with just the vaguest cognitive hint, he eventually surrendered the point. 'You should have your own television show, you're so full of shit.'

My heart leapt. It had been so long since someone said something even remotely vitriolic to me that it took a couple of seconds for the cobwebs to clear in that part of my brain that had lain dormant since I was a teenager. Before the accident, it had been the entirety of my exterior communications. I covered my thinking with a smile, then folded my arms. 'Yeah, well, at least my shit is a self-sustainable addiction.'

I could tell he was impressed. 'My, we have become tough.'

He was so full of himself and his self-image that I wanted to shred his ego to pieces and watch him wiggle like a beetle on its back. No – one straight look at him, and that wasn't what I wanted to do at all. He was much too attractive, in an ugly kind of way. I would rather shred the clothes off him and watch him wiggle on his back – or mine.

'You think this is tough? It's ten in the morning. Come back later in the night. I'll show you tough.'

'I'd rather you showed me a good time.'

Yes, he was impressed. But he was also notoriously cruel. I scrubbed the visions of him wiggling on my back when I heard Brendan careering down the stairs like an oversized kid.

Brendan loved Shane, judging by the way he was hanging off every mumbled word. If he had a tail, he would have wagged it. I climbed the staircase with Kyle to watch the family reunion, in an attempt to stave off the nausea. Hanging over the side of the balcony, we could see the tops of their heads and their faces as they performed some strange kind of male bonding ritual. Most of the hugging and talking came from Brendan, whose eyes held that strange glimmer of anticipation normally restricted to scoring drugs. And when Shane said he was going to be in town for a while, doing a course, the glimmer turned into mild hysteria. Brendan exclaimed. Kyle and I looked at each other and winked in a more controlled hysteria.

With Kyle's grapevine connections, it wasn't hard to get the lowdown on Shane. One story mentioned trouble with a black magic cult. Another cited heroin as correspondent. There was talk of woman problems, man problems, cop problems and family problems. Nothing new for Shane, Kyle reckoned, recounting with excited eyes and tongue the time that a girl Brendan was in love with decided she liked Shane better and whammo! Brendan saw them at the Ballroom together one night and completely exploded. Within a couple of weeks, Shane had tired of the girl, called Caroline, who in the meantime had become a junkie with galloping consumption. He ditched her. She turned up dead of an overdose in the front yard of the house they all shared. Brendan went crazy. Shane tried to kill himself. In an ironic twist, Brendan walked in on Shane after he'd taken his nice big dose and saved his life. They'd never been the same since, Kyle reckoned, but they never were in the first place. I stared, overwhelmed at the drama of it all. She smiled, glad to have imparted it. Gossip served a very real purpose. It took us a few steps back from reality. A hot, desperate reality. Surviving the heat of the day meant survival of the laziest. That's what Kyle would say, anyway, scratching her nose, half on the nod.

Myself, I didn't need any artificial encouragement to be lazy. The lazy dog usually gets the quick brown fox in the end.

CHAPTER FIVE

Natural selection

Ryders was my favourite bar, because it was free on week nights, and it was just around the corner from home. Sly and I could get as drunk as our bodies would allow us on the suspicious house moselle, make fools of ourselves on the dance floor, request the most tragic disco songs from the DJ, whose record collection ended in 1978 but whose favourite band were the Dead Kennedys, then stagger home in a breeze and collapse in bed, often in each other's. There was a time when I thought I was falling in love with Sly. He was the perfect social companion. I could say whatever I wanted, and although he would say, 'Oh, if only Brendan could hear you say that!' he wouldn't repeat it. We would huddle in dark corner tables and watch the parade of men from across the coloured dance floor, speculate and fantasise, but not do much else.

Sly's rampant promiscuity came to an abrupt end when he found out that an ex-lover had come down with AIDS. After a horrendous few days, when he was so sure he was going to waste away and die that he was too scared to leave his room, I convinced him to have a test. Arm in arm, we went to the Prince Henry hospital, where several days later he was pronounced negative, but told to come back in three months for the second test, to be sure. On Holy Tuesday, the second test was still six weeks away, and Sly was still deep-down scared. I tried to tell him that if he used safe sex practices there was little or no risk, but he wouldn't have it. It was almost as if the mere thought of sex would bring hell and damnation, and the four-letter disease, down on him. Sly was becoming a victim of guilt and media hype. It was just like the old 'Smiley' song – 'No more laughter in the air, feel the tension in the air' – I was sweating on Sly's test almost as much as he was. In this kind of situation, there was only one thing to do. When the going gets tough . . . the tough camp it up.

And so we came to be dancing down Smith Street at 2 AM singing a Boney M medley. This was a highly unfashionable thing to do at the time, but we were safe in the assumption that everyone we knew would be either asleep, or at a big street party up in North Fitzroy.

'She's crazy for you, Daddy – oooh, she believes in you – she loves her Daddy – '

Sly's baritone had improved since he last sang with Brendan and Dominic's band. He screeched for thirty-five minutes then, until his voice had disappeared completely. When it had returned, several days later, it was several octaves deeper.

'She's crazy like a fool, about Daddy Cool – '

My voice had never been that good, but it didn't seem to matter, as the empty street's shop awnings supplied an echo, and the sun-parched bitumen lapped it up. Sly gyrated on a rubbish bin, then did an amazing dive, catching a No Standing sign on his way down and swinging around like a monkey. I squealed in appreciation and was about to try something similar, albeit on a smaller scale with a fire hydrant when, like some weird kind of hallucinatory ghost, Shane Brophy appeared.

I screamed out of shock. Sly screamed, whooping it up.

'Hello, Caitlin,' Shane said with an arrogant undertone, the face devoid of expression. In my state, I barely believed he was real. I looked at Sly, as if he could tell me if I was hallucinating, and he dug me in the ribs and whispered, 'Looks like you're luck's come in!' Then, before I could stop him, he was running off up the street, singing 'I'm a star in New York, I'm a star in LA – '

The street became deathly silent. It was a complete social shock, one minute whooping it up with Sly, next minute alone in a hot, dry street with Shane.

'Isn't this a funny coincidence?' I asked, walking a circle around him in an attempt to look contrived, when it was only because I couldn't walk a straight line. 'You materialising – amazing! Or did you have another dream? Or are you some kind of astral hologram beamed from some murky Sydney backwater?' I finished my circle, and scrutinised his face. 'You could be quite palatable, in an anarcho-nihilist pre-apocalyptic chic kind of way, if you weren't such an arrogant son of a bitch.'

He almost smiled, before taking a step back and saying, 'Please excuse me, I thought I was talking to a human being.'

'A human being? Get real, this is Fitzroy.'

His smile could have been real. Most likely, it was patronising. The offer to walk me home was real enough though, despite being qualified as a public safety service.

Sounds denoting 'party' met us at the corner of my street. The street party up in North Fitzroy had materialised outside my place. People were across the footpath, on the road, turning on all the hoses and wetting down the bitumen which heated up the city like heat-storing elements on a huge electric grill. It may have been two, but no one seemed to mind. It was so hot, no one would be able to sleep without drugging themselves with beer or pills or smack or sex or work or late-night movies.

'Told you I could show you a good time,' I said to Shane as we wound our way through the people along the wrought-iron fence to my front gate. 'You see, this is how it's done.'

He glanced around at a couple kissing, someone rolling a joint, Dominic and Mad Lenny slamming Tequila in huge Vegemite jars, and someone else losing bladder control and consciousness on my window sill.

'Oh, I don't know,' he said thoughtfully, 'Looks a little conventional to me.'

Yes. I watched them, and wondered why I hadn't realised before. They were specialised yobbos. A peculiar strain. Brendan came out to meet us, a walking mass of flesh, blood and heroin. He was so out of it that he could hardly walk. Almost tip-toeing, smooth, clumsy, he greeted us enthusiastically and then threw up all over my dress. I screamed and kicked him, and everyone seemed to think it was hilarious, even me, although I had to feign outrage for the duration of the show.

'I'm going to change,' I told Shane, ignoring Brendan as he worked hard on his new image.

'Can I watch?'

Of course he didn't watch, and I was glad of it. He was all talk, just like me. I changed into an oversized singlet while he looked through a box of art prints I'd found in an alley that afternoon. He kept unrolling them and saying 'Oh, Mondrian!' and 'Oh, Chagall!' in a cool voice that belied his delight. I thought it was very strange the way he repressed all emotion. But then, it's a strange kind of world, and keeping a straight face is as good a defence as any other.

'So, Bucko,' I said when I had composed myself with a glass of cheap cask moselle, 'got any smack on you?'

He'd been daydreaming, looking at a low-quality print of Chagall's 'Green Violinist'. Sly had picked it out while I was getting ready for the Club, and hinted heavily that it would look great in his room. Tomorrow, I would give it to him.

It took me a few moments in my inebriated state to realise that Shane was staring at me, appalled, as if I'd suggested a little spot of cannibalism.

'What?' The green violinist dangled in distracted hands.

'Don't play innocent.'

'Don't call me Bucko.'

'Well, what d'ya say?'

'No way.'

I detected a tinge of haughtiness. 'Why not? I'll pay: you can have a commission.'

'It's Jordan. And Roman. And Brendan. And Kit too. They'd all kill me.' He really did have a sense of humour in there, somewhere behind the straight face.

'They can't all kill you,' I said calmly.

'Don't you bet on it. Kit would find a way to resurrect me if she could, to have another crack.'

'Oh,' I said, climbing closer to him with the offer of a drink, 'you don't get on with your mother?'

He almost laughed, despite himself. I zoned in on the chink in the permafrost and said, 'Come on, between you and me, I'm curious about all things, including drugs, but if I say anything to Brendan and Kyle, they'll get hysterical. It pleases their conscience to have me innocent, as it were.'

Taking a glass of moselle from my hand, he watched me for a few moments in a manner not particularly pleasant.

I had the feeling that I was being examined. He took a deep breath and said, 'Well, never let it be said I passed up a chance to corrupt innocence.'

I held my glass out to his. 'Tomorrow?'

He clicked his against mine. 'Tomorrow.'

I sat down opposite him and looked at the 'Green Violinist'. I was beginning to feel a shade of green myself, owing to too much wine and not enough food. Outside my window, a couple of people were arguing over a stubbie of Coopers.

'I used to play violin,' Shane said off-handedly, just a touch of sentiment seeping through.

'Used to? So what happened?'

He shrugged. 'I got too lazy.'

I nodded in silent, thoughtful affirmation. I knew that one for a fact. 'I have a theory about laziness, and survival of the fittest,' I said. 'But I can't be bothered telling you.'

He watched me for a while, and I watched him for a while longer, because he fell asleep before I did. With his eyes closed, he didn't look half as threatening. He was a survivor, completely adapted.

CHAPTER SIX

Ash

It was Ash Wednesday, and incredibly hot. All the oxygen seemed to have been sucked away violently, and I imagined the nuclear fireball poised to scorch us at any moment. I thought about nuclear war a lot. More than some, not as much as others. The mushroom cloud was carved as deep in my psyche as daisies and teddy bears. It was the godfather I never had: my family and my security. My fear and my loathing.

'You should see it,' Kyle said breathlessly as she emerged, covered in sweat, from a venture outdoors. 'From the top floor of the social security building, you can see everything. The whole horizon has got a red aura. It's really creepy out there. Got anything planned?'

I smiled to myself, and said, 'Perhaps. What would you suggest, weather like this?'

She didn't have to think about it at all. 'Procure a good-looking man and some drugs, then draw all the curtains. I tell you, this is not a good day. I'm about as psychic as a concrete slab, but I can feel it.' She noted a noise from the hallway, and peeked through the door. 'Shane's here. There's one half of the equation.'

A sick din arose in my stomach. The one that always said, Are you sure you know what you're doing? The one that feels like acid burning the stomach lining. I gulped down some wine then dashed into the shower.

It was late in the afternoon before I actually got around to talking to Shane. He was playing some kind of possum, giving me cryptic looks but nothing else. Cornered by a drunken Brendan armed with his photo collection, Shane looked at pictures of himself until he was very grey in the face. Or could it be that he was hanging out? Whatever, I couldn't take my eyes off him.

Brendan and Dominic and the boys from their band decided to sit out the heat at an air-conditioned watering hole. Kyle, despairing at Shane's complete lack of interest, was going to call in on an old lover. Marcie had been gone for a couple of days. She was probably on Mars.

'Well, Bucko,' I said when we were finally alone, 'you took your time.'

He took a long look around the destruction in the lounge-room. No-one had cleaned up in a few days, and it was a health hazard. 'If you call me Bucko once more,' he said slowly, with a smile in his voice.

'What? Ha? What'll you do? You're all talk.'

The sun was beginning to go down. It looked like the

beginning of the end of the world.

He put his index finger where the needle had plunged in and out, then folded up my elbow. Shane was a smooth operator, and he had a smooth touch. His fingers gently massaged my inner elbow, as if to help the opiates on their way.

A second or two, and then a wave of loosely panicked unreality hit me, like instant drunkenness. Suddenly nothing worried me: not the oppressive heat, not his repressive reservation, not anything. From the back of my neck, down my arms and through my body, a dull, cool nausea spread in waves, all consuming.

'Okay?'

I didn't realise my eyes were closed, and when I realised, I didn't care – I nodded, or waved my hand, some kind of affirmation, then closed my mind in ecstasy. The trams on Victoria Street sounded like waves crashing on a beach – they were waves, crashing on a cool, windy beach. The nature of reality had changed to a personal selection.

Shane had his back to me, and I could see all of his bones, shoulder blades and ribs sticking out from under the (black, naturally) T-shirt. I left the chair and floated down to the floor next to him, watching him injecting himself. It struck me as very brutal and honest, and as uncompromising as the collection of marks on his inner elbow. The methodical, surgical process, then the reward: his expression didn't change but his eyes did. They became soft and glassy. The muscles of his body relaxed. His lungs relaxed, and exhaled deeply. I really had to check myself because I was beginning to think and feel things that could get me into trouble.

'You look like I feel,' I said.

As he packed up the works, he said, 'You must be stoned.'

I was. Crashingly. But I couldn't help thinking, Right, what comes next? Or was I just expecting too much? It was only a drug. Beneath the euphoria, I was still myself.

'This is heroin?' I said, while the drug soothed every vein and muscle in my throat.

He rolled the throw-aways in newspaper then deposited them in my rubbish bin. Settling down on the floor opposite me, he gave me an intoxicated half-smile and said, 'Yeah. What do you think?'

'Oh – ' I tried hard not to look at him. In vain. 'Seems to turn off rather than turn on. Nice.'

'But not worth getting a habit over?'

What did he want, criticism? A fight? No, he looked too lazy. I leant across and flicked on the radio. 'That's not for me to say.' Light dance music began to fill the air waves. 'You're a smart boy. I'd say you take care of your own business. I would also guess that buried way down there' – I leant forward and dug an imaginary hole in his fine shapen forehead with my index finger – 'lurks a sensitive soul, too timid or too smart to come out. Which is perfectly understandable. If I had a sensitive soul, I wouldn't let it anywhere near me.'

'You're perfectly right.' He was smiling.

'Don't agree with me!'

'Why not? How far are you going to take this?'

'What?'

He leant right forward, so our heads were almost touching. 'Do I get to stay here and indulge my masochist fetish via the delectable lashes of your tongue, or do I have to go so that no one will be compromised?'

I studied his face for a moment. I bet he looked incredible when he came. That thought alone was enough to seal it. Of course he would stay. I wouldn't send my worst enemy out in this weather, let alone a guy who looked like he wanted to eat me. Oh, yes, I wanted to be compromised.

Shane came back with a damp flannel and, as he wiped it down my face, neck and chest with more than a little erotic innuendo, he musically intoned, 'Outside, the air is full of black smoke and ash. It's Ash Wednesday, you know: either it's an irrefutable sign that there IS a God who keeps the Roman calender, or there's an enormous fire somewhere.'

He'd never said so much at one time without provocation. I said, 'My money's on the fire.' He bent down and kissed me where the flannel had been, his mouth murmuring muffled things into the soft flesh of my breast. I listened to it, felt it, and decided then and there that I would never forget this, as long as I lived.

Suddenly, there was a knocking on the door, and I heard Brendan's voice say, 'Eh, Cait, are you – ' as the door opened. If only it had been locked.

Brendan appeared, smiling and a little sunburnt. He saw Shane, then me, and went pale and silent.

A huge, hot cloud filled the air. All life stopped for a split second. I was naked: Shane had jeans on, but he was in a compromising position. I heard him mutter 'Fuck' into my skin. A bead of sweat rolled off his forehead, onto my nipple. Right on impact, the room seemed to spontaneously combust.

It happened too quickly for my slowed-down brain to register. Before I could blink, Brendan had hold of Shane by the face and was slamming the back of his head into the wall above the fireplace. They were both yelling, and I was probably yelling too, because it seemed a dead certainty that Brendan was trying to cause serious injury, or death. I dragged the sheet off my bed and threw it over Brendan's head then gathered it in quickly, just like I had seen in a movie recently. It controlled the arm movements for a couple of seconds. Long enough for Shane to jump away and stand there looking as if his brain had been pulverised.

'Bastard!' Brendan yelled, pulling the sheet off with extreme violence, 'You're finished!'

He didn't look at me. Not even as he smashed everything on the dressing table on the way out.

Shane was obviously shaken. He locked the door then bent his forehead against the wood. Fine shaped forehead, pressed against the grain. I didn't think about anything else. It was too hot. I looked at the digital clock.

'That'll be the seven o'clock compromise.'

He looked at me briefly, then continued his short focus on the wood grain. I knew it was up to me to save this situation. If I wanted to save it.

'Fuck,' was all he said.

'All right,' I said, as if he'd been asking me. He looked at me slowly, as if he no longer knew me. I slid out of the bed and said, 'Reality's gonna come in with a sledgehammer soon enough.'

He was shaking his head. 'There's things that you don't know.'

'I know, I know, I went through a state school system. There's things I don't know, but I know what I like. And let's face it' – I stood face to face with him, but to do this I had to stand on a milk crate and look down slightly – 'we're here, and it's hot outside.'

'And you're naked.' He slid his hands around my hips, a thin veil of sweat cooling the motion.

'And I don't care.' I kissed him.

'I know. That's what I love about you.'

He said the 'L' word. Perhaps a slip of the tongue: perhaps

a symptom of the heat. Next thing I knew, he had lifted me up, against the door to the outside world, the heat and Brendan's torment, other people's preconceptions and double standards, and we fucked them all to oblivion.

Late in the night, I opened the window. Hot air and ash blew in. We climbed through and walked out into the night. The street lights blared down on a reddy-brown haze. The delicatessen, the bottle shop, the cars and trams, all figments of some kind of dream. We bought enough supplies, we figured, so that we could hole up and hide out for a few days. Only we didn't feel like eating, and most of the wine was lost when Shane poured it over me and attempted to lick it up. Most of what he did was kinky, in one way or another, although it didn't seem strange at the time. The only thing out of place seemed to be conversation. So when he said 'Caitlin' with that look in his eyes that meant SERIOUS, I buried his head hard into my breasts. I knew he loved that. He didn't try and talk any more.

CHAPTER SEVEN

Peer

I was almost at the end before I realised I'd never been on a pier before, and I damn well didn't like it. All I could picture was the power of the waves, the mass of water, and me standing on this matchstick contraption in the midst of it. Images of piers destroyed by storms filled my mind, and I began to feel it sway, the water swirling beneath the boards. Would the next one break, plunging me downwards? Surely it would. Out on a pier, and I couldn't swim. The distance I'd walked to place myself in this perilous situation stretched before me like a long, flat, endless country road. No visible means of support.

Feeling like a goon at the age of ten. Younger kids splashing around me in the dam. Caitlin too scared to go near the edge.

'It's really easy,' Sally was saying. Sally was James's girlfriend at the time. She had four bratty kids, and believed she could solve the problems of the world. 'I'll take you in.' No thanks. Sally wasn't fat, but she looked really heavy, as if her bones were made of lead. An image of her sinking like a stone, taking me in with her . . .

'Leave her alone,' James ended up saying. He had a few flecks of grey in his beard then. 'She doesn't like to swim.' Good old James. He could always be counted on to back me up, no matter what. Long as I could remember, he made me responsible for my own actions, and took responsibility accordingly.

'But EVERYONE likes to swim! Perhaps she drowned in a past life, and that's why.'

Ten years on, I had a better idea of why I didn't like big masses of water, but I still didn't like to swim. Any amateur Jungian would say the same thing: fear of the unknown. Fear of the unconscious. I knew that if I wanted to swim, I'd be a dolphin. Sure, they went back to the water, but they had millions of years of evolution on their side. I only had a pale pink body with flailing arms, taking in too much water, bloating up like a balloon.

When Shane finally arrived – almost an hour late – I let him have it. Sadistic bastard. I supposed he thought it was funny to have me hanging around on a windy pier like some desperate whore from a bad old movie. Very funny. Hilarious.

'You don't like water, then?' he said, handing me a chocolate bar I had no intention of eating, as if it were nothing, when at that moment it felt like certain death.

'No. And I can't bloody swim!'

'Neither can I.'

This was supposed to be some kind of consolation. Almost screaming by now, I let him know that although I had recently and perhaps mistakenly come to look on him as some kind of friend, there was no way on earth that I wanted to die with him.

Seagulls started squawking overhead. Shane's skin was pale: he'd stopped walking. 'If you don't want to die with me,' he said, 'then there's nothing to talk about.'

I'd lost him by that stage. I had no idea of what he was on about, and I was too rattled to care. Backing away towards the shore, I yelled, 'Good! Have a nice day!' He stood there staring at me as if it meant nothing.

By the time I got to shore, I was completely depressed. I tried not to think too much: I decided to write Shane off to experience. I should have known not to hang out with someone crazier than me. From the Mr Whippy van I got a chocolate-coated Dairy Queen and seagull shit on my shoulder.

Anyone would have thought I'd dropped the Zyklon B into the showers, or did the hard sell on Eve with the apple, or lit the Ash Wednesday fires. No one would talk to me. Even people I didn't know gave me foul looks when I walked through the lounge-room. Dominic was the first one to have a go at me about Brendan being too upset to practise with the band. The other two guys stood in the doorway like executioners. I took a look around the lounge-room full of hardcore boys with their images to sustain and told Dominic to go and screw his mother.

Kyle appeared then in the struggle to keep Dominic from strangling me, and dragged me up the hall, yelling that I should know better than to say anything to Dominic about his mother. She was jealous because I'd managed to fuck the Iceman when she hadn't. Even Sly was jealous, because I'd had hard drugs without cutting him in.

I didn't see Brendan for two days. And when I did, he wouldn't talk to me. So I waited until one afternoon when they were all in the lounge-room, then I marched in and told them it would be better for everyone if I moved out. I stared at Brendan until he couldn't avoid me any more. When his eyes finally connected with mine, I realised he was more embarrassed than anything else. He shook his head, picked up his jacket, took hold of my arm and led me straight out through the kitchen door, the back door, the back gate, down the alley, along the street, to the pub.

We didn't talk until we both had drinks in our hands. And then Brendan asked me point blank, 'So what, you still seeing him?' I shook my head. This seemed to be enough for him. We downed a few drinks, talked about the bushfires and other disasters and then, when Brendan had reached his preferred level of drunkenness, he started telling me that it was all Shane's fault anyway. He enjoyed hurting people, screwing them around, watching the outcome, because he was a complete emotional cripple. Had been for as long as they'd known each other. There was something cruel and bitter and very final about the way Brendan said, 'One day, someone will come along and get him back. REALLY get him back.'

Out of necessity, I managed to push the whole sordid thing from my mind and block out the hurt and embarrassment, through drink and drugs and anything else that was on hand. Several months passed in a complete dream.

I even tried to fall in love. Someone – anyone – would have sufficed, but no matter how hard I tried, or Kyle tried for me in her cupid capacity, I could never get past a one-night stand. And there were no shortage of takers for these, since the word had got around about me and Shane. Men who never gave me a second glance were now buying me drinks. I would get as drunk as I could in the hope that it would mean something. But it never did. And when the news came to me via a letter from Roman that Shane had gone to India to work on his drug habit, it signalled the final dissolution of optimism. I had my friends, my flatmates, my peers: I was alone.

A curious thing happened around the middle of 1983. Like a weird kind of virus. Ninety per cent of the people I knew developed heroin habits of one degree or another.

It was upon them before they realised. Social users became every day users. They started draining their dregs. All sorts of disgusting things. Not to say that I have never done a disgusting thing, but if I did, it was out of desire. Brendan, Kyle, Marcie, Dominic and the others were becoming obsessed with it. I observed them in this way, and it gave me the encouragement not to become an addict. If I ever found myself needing more to get out of it, I forced myself to leave it alone for a while. Nevertheless, I did rage out with them regularly.

Brendan and Marcie had met an amiable dealer named John the Score who never fucked them around. He was a diamond in the heroin scene and he was rewarded with a flourishing business. So I heard. I never met any of these people myself. Being the essentially trusting, not to mention lazy, person that I was, I always just handed the money over to Brendan and Marcie and let them do the business. I didn't want the stress. But then little by little, taste by taste, it began to dawn on me.

Someone would only have to mention scoring and half-a-dozen minds would start ticking over, a psychic disease spreading throughout, until we ended up scraping together what we could. At least we were still at that stage, of sharing. A few records sold here, a radio hocked there, borrowed money in desperation and then an immense feeling of relief when, at last, it was affordable. If it wasn't, we would all sulk in our rooms separately. It was maddening. A terrible, maudlin kind of madness.

A girl named Cathy used to come around from time to time, with the sole purpose of making us hang out. Then, when we were itching enough to want to score and had already sold our grandmothers to pay for it, Cathy would hover around like a chemical cloud, then hit with lines like 'Can I buy two dollars worth off you?' or 'Can I have your dregs?' There was nothing she wouldn't do for a hit. She was the personification of the disease. It was her job to spread it. That way, she had more sources.

Brendan found a way to pay her back. He would go and visit her in her empty, dirty dive and make out that he'd just had a taste; sniffing, scratching, nodding off severely. Cathy would just about go through the roof. It was cruel, perhaps, but Cathy was worse. She never recognised, or admitted, her own weakness. She knew not what she did. Her mind only had one track, and it was slow.

Of all the people I had met in Melbourne, besides Kyle and Brendan, my favourite was Dekkar. He was from Sydney, and from the moment he arrived, in the depths of winter, life became a lot easier. A lot more secure. He was one of those people who could talk to anyone about anything. Impassioned, intelligent, built like a brick wall with tattoos and shaven head to boot, he looked like a heavy thug and loved Cocteau films. One of those rare breeds – a living legend who actually lived up to the stories. Wild accounts of partying, chasing fascist skinheads, drug taking and comradeship. He was different from most of the other guys in that he didn't seem to have anything to prove. He was comfortable with himself, and he acted accordingly. He told me I should be more comfortable with myself. Yes, some stories had spread to Sydney about my rampant behaviour after the Ash Wednesday fires, picking fights with Dominic, throwing jugs of beer onto people, pulling a knife on Mad Lenny Murchison. I told him I never pulled a knife on Mad Lenny: it was a screwdriver covered with bong scrapings. Never mind, he said, I should not quell my spirit just to conform.

I thought about this for a long time, then told him that if my mouth said everything that my brain wanted it to, I'd be dead within a week. He laughed and told me not to underestimate people. Okay, I said, within a day. Dekkar laughed. He promised to back me up if I said or did anything which someone else couldn't handle. He was serious, some kind of home-boy zen master of self-expression and non-conformity. Dekkar was fine.

Kyle and I still managed to raise the energy, optimism and make-up semi-regularly to go out nightclubbing like we used to. Dancing was the only real exercise I got these days, since Sly's test results came back positive and he decided to get all serious and healthy and concentrate on his art. I still saw him daily, but the rapport had changed. I was living, according to him, a very dangerous life. He made me promise never to share needles and always use condoms. As the word got around about him, everyone started taking more care. To an extent. If they were desperate for a hit or a fuck, thoughts of a way-off disease didn't enter into it. It was, after all, 1983. We were all sure we were going to fry in a nuclear war. The only thing we could do to stop it was party.

We went out on Saturdays when Brendan and Dominic's band weren't playing to a club in the city which played mostly English dance music. Brendan and Dominic called us 'Trendies'. Kyle would say, 'As long as I'm an immensely attractive Trendy, who cares?' We dragged them along one night.

Dominic was visibly uncomfortable, not sure about all these men wearing dark eye shadow. He went out to the street, down half a block and around into a back alley to avoid going into the Gents. He was quite repressed. Brendan, on the other hand, was immediately relaxed. He kept running into middle-class Eastern suburbs types he went to the Grammar with. His mohican appearance made him like a magnet: he was the hit of the evening. Girls (and a couple of boys) kept trying to take him home.

We split from Dominic and Kyle and went for a walk around that part of the CBD; Saturday night walkers never failing to stare unabashed at him, jovial in his erect mohawk. With anyone else I would have made a Freudian joke, but Brendan wasn't really that sort of guy. For all his worldliness, in his heart he was still a clean-cut boy from Glen Waverley.

We'd become best friends. It was as if Ash Wednesday had never happened. It was impossible. If, as Kyle said, Brendan had been 'besotted' with me (and I'd always had my doubts there, as there was no real justification) then he certainly wasn't now. When we came to Elizabeth Street, he was lamenting the loss of a phone number – Little Alison from the Dead Kennedys' gig. At the corner of Flinders Street, in front of the seventies kitsch Commonwealth Bank, we stood telling jokes and laughing at the thought of Dominic back at the club. Laughing at nothing, really. Just laughing. We thought we'd get a taxi home, then try and rustle up some smack from a guy called Al with a beeper who did housecalls.

At the taxi rank opposite the Commonwealth Bank and all its black marble, we ate greasy chips and waited for one of the rare vehicles to come along. There must have been a taxi driver strike or something, because we seemed to wait forever. Music was going around in my head, heart still going in time to the drum machines. I must have been drunk because I was dancing to 'Lust for Life', which was playing in my head. Then the taxi came. Brendan steered me towards it as I sang, '"I'm worth a million prizes."' I have a terrible voice, and he was covering my mouth in an attempt to keep himself from cracking up when the back door of the taxi opened, and out came first a loosely packed sports bag, then, of all things, Shane Brophy.

We all saw each other at once. That's probably why it

didn't go down in the history of diplomacy and foreign relations. Brendan and Shane were completely mute. I cut the ice by involuntarily exclaiming, 'Jesus H. Christ and his black bastard brother!'

Brendan turned and looked at me as if he'd never heard me say anything worse than 'bottom'. When I connected with Shane, he was wearing an expression I recognised instantly. It was the way he'd looked when we saw 'Eraserhead'. As if he was going to collapse and form a black hole at any moment.

'Of all the taxis, huh?'

Was this his attempt at humour? Shit, it didn't matter.

Brendan turned and walked away. I had no choice but to follow.

It was a pretty rough half hour before Al arrived. We sat in the kitchen in oppressed silence, punctuated by Brendan pacing up and down, squashing food scraps into the disgusting linoleum. That's all I was really thinking about, the mess someone was going to have to scrape off the floor tomorrow. Or, knowing our household, next time someone was up all night on speed. That's the only time things like floor and bathroom cleaning were even attempted. The silence in the kitchen was glaring. It was a really bad, bad scene. Brendan's face wasn't just cloudy. It was cyclonic.

And then, the relief. The sound of Al's car. A big Valiant, so it blew a fanfare. We looked each other in the eye. It was the last time we looked at each other that night.

Sunday brunch. Brendan was still up in his room. Marcie and I sat at the kitchen table, cutting Jungle Buddies from the back of a Coco Pops packet. Kyle came breezing in from the back door, still dressed and made up for Saturday night. It was funny, but 'All Tomorrow's Parties' just happened to be on the radio.

'Caitlin!' She started on me immediately, before even sitting down. 'You'll never believe who turned up at Todd's place last night.'

I took one guess. 'The Iceman.'

She was stunned. 'How did you know?'

'Oh, I heard it on the grapevine.' She was still standing there, expectantly. I pushed Marcie's feet off the chair and said, 'Sit down and tell us about it, then.' Not that Kyle ever needed encouragement to deliver news.

'He looks REALLY different,' she babbled with the edginess of one coming down off speed, 'though he said he spent three months out of it in Amsterdam, so that's understandable.'

'You spoke to him, I take it.'

'Yeah. I've – uh – just come from his place.' I looked up at her silently, quizzically, thinking, You – and Shane? She smiled at me for a moment. She knew my game. Patting my shoulder, she said, 'Don't worry, Caitlin, I didn't open my legs all night.'

I stifled a smile. 'My only worry is your vulgarity.'

'How did you go to the dunny?' Marcie asked. We ignored her.

'Are you interested?' Kyle asked me. She already knew the answer. She just wanted me to suffer the indignity of acquiescing.

'Yeah.' I heard a movement from upstairs, and added, 'But you'd better make it the abridged version, cos Brendan's due any time.'

'Abridged? Little place on Rathdowne Street, near the commission flats. Looks like he lives there on his own – it's pretty neat.' She glanced around the kitchen and sniffed disapprovingly. 'I don't know what his game is, though. He gave me a full-on spiel about safe sex, and ten packets of condoms.' She emptied them out of her bag onto the kitchen table. 'He said to make sure I gave a box to you.'

'Charming,' I grumbled.

'And he wanted me to give you his address' – she pulled a crumpled note from the melee of her handbag – 'and this.' From her pocket she extracted a second note. As it touched my palm, she held my hand for a second and said, 'Better get there quick, before the undertakers do.'

A fine way to start the morning. From the staircase, we heard the unmistakeable sound of Brendan's Doc Martens negotiating the stairs. I shoved the papers into my pockets, and the three of us were trying to hide the condoms when Brendan came into the room. He was his bright, cheerful self.

'Ah, the three witches!'

'"Bubble bubble, toil and trouble,"' I recited.

Marcie looked around and said, 'No, "Snap, crackle and pop!"' Kyle and I looked at each other, but decided it would be cruel to laugh.

'What's this?' Brendan picked up a packet of condoms. We all looked at each other as if to say, 'He doesn't know?'

Kyle snatched the packet from him and said, 'It's my daily supply.'

I read the note in the bathroom.

'Just so you know, I don't regret anything.'

I stared out of the window, right into Sly's back yard. He was entertaining a friend, playing his Noel Coward record to the whole neighbourhood. 'Don't put your daughter on the stage, Mrs Worthington, don't put your daughter on the stage.'

I screwed up the note and the address, after they were committed to memory. To history.

CHAPTER EIGHT

If one green bottle should accidentally fall

November and December marched along playfully. We had a union, Brendan, Dekkar, Kyle and I, that was nigh on a full-blown four-sided relationship. We did everything together. It was always a case of 'What will *we* do today?', or 'How can *we* get the money to score?' Our dole cheques were distributed through the fortnight period so that one of us always had money. We shared everything, except needles. Because we had each other, and a constant, albeit tiny, amount of money, we weren't prey to a lot of the ugliness that surrounded us. We didn't lock ourselves in the bathroom like Marcie did to have a hit. Careful not to tempt anyone who wanted to lay off, we made sure no-one was left wanting. So the story went. Really we were justifying each other's drug binges. A kind of communal habit-sharing.

On Brendan's birthday, I went with him out to Glen Waverley, heart of the suburban sprawl, and had lunch with his parents. They seemed nice enough; had even given him a car as a birthday present. It was a second-hand Lancer, but it was mobility. I couldn't help thinking that if they were so nice, why did they shove him away in a boarding school for so many years? He always said he didn't mind, really, but I could tell, from seeing him with them just for that lunch, that he longed to be a kid again. To be THEIR kid. They liked it the way it was. Kindness for appearance's sake. They gave me a present – a sub-atomic bottle of Chanel No. 5 – and I acted suitably grateful. And then Brendan took the keys to the Lancer and we drove up to the Dandenong Hills, talking the whole time about our childhoods and experiences during puberty and all the most excruciating things. Although I didn't tell him about Cal, and he didn't tell me about Caroline. I thought to myself, If it's ever going to happen between Brendan and me, it will be now. But it wasn't to be. We just drove around for a while, then straight back down the highway to town. By the time we got to Fitzroy, I knew that while he was not my boyfriend, he was my best friend.

If November was playful, then December was risky. Long-shots were the call of the day. Kyle fell head-over-heels for a guy named Michael who did everything but reciprocate her feelings. It was her first disappointment ever, and she crashed very heavily. Dekkar was crashing too, although his problems stemmed from drugs, not love. In an attempt to go cold turkey, he made himself so sick that he ended up in hospital, almost dead from malnutrition and some kind of salt deficiency. Brendan refused to go to the hospital to see him, suffering his own kind of collapse. He'd recently undergone a drug problem of a different kind: out scoring with Marcie one night, they inadvertently got involved with one of the St Kilda police's Saturday night roundups. Back at the station, a search produced the smack. Brendan and Marcie were separated, and he copped a possession charge. Marcie, however, copped it sweet. She was on the nod within half an hour of getting home later that night, so Brendan assumed she'd done some sort of deal with the cops. This surprised none of us except Brendan, who started getting paranoid about everyone. He put a padlock on his bedroom door, a sign not to just Marcie but the rest of us as well. I seemed to be the only one in control. Which was just as well, as everyone else needed special treatment.

It was another hot December afternoon: close enough to Christmas for the decorations to be up around the wards. Dekkar was squeezed in a public ward, between a man with a serious bowel complaint who was forever emitting noxious fumes, and a younger guy who just wanted to talk and talk and talk. Kyle and I wheeled Dekkar out onto the balcony, where we sat and watched the traffic pouring into the city. One thing that Kyle's beau Michael was good for was killer weed: sweet, spicy-smelling buddha. Smoking it seemed a desecration. It should have been a cologne.

Dekkar was getting philosophical in his old age (twenty-five). The whole experience was not lost on him: he said he wouldn't be going back to smack. Not until a fair amount of time had elapsed, anyway. Kyle and I squirmed uncomfortably on the hospital lounges, for neither of us was game to cut out the main respite from life. The pleasure of life. And Dekkar was not exactly a walking advertisement for kicking the habit.

'When I get out of here,' he told us with the dumb grin he always assumed when stoned, 'which will be the day after tomorrow, hopefully – I've been thinking of moving in with Shane.'

Kyle and I looked at each other, and she burst into a snort of laughter and said, 'Isn't that laying temptation all over the path?'

Dekkar did admit that it seemed a bit silly. 'Oh, he doesn't use smack any more. His next door neighbour is a naturopath: she's got some kind of homeopathic methadone thing brewing up.' He repositioned himself in the wheelchair and said, 'I need peace and quiet for a while. Lots of good food and grass.'

We left when it was drug trolley time: exiting the ward, my bag happened to catch onto the curtain surrounding the poor man with the bowel complaint. As I walked along, it pulled the curtain wide open to reveal him, according to Kyle, poised on a bedpan. It was grotesque and hilarious, although we held off the laughter until we were near the lifts. Nervous chortles kept us empowered until we shot downstairs, went through the labyrinth lobby and out onto the street, the stench of the methane and the disinfectant following us all the way home to Fitzroy.

I was watching television among the empties, old newspapers and cigarettes with parts of their filters pulled out, when the sounds of voices yelling at each other reached me along the empty echo chambers of our hallway. Brendan and Kyle were at it again. When they had arguments, they made sure the whole block knew about it. I tried to close in focus on the television – afternoon soap opera, never very good for concentration – until the shouts came down the stairs, along the hall, into the lounge-room. Brendan was steaming along, huffing and puffing, with Kyle following close behind, arms flying about, giving me that look that says, All men are crazy.

In five seconds, I knew the score. Brendan had just found out that Dekkar was going to move in with Shane, and he was furious. He wanted to go to the hospital and tell Dekkar no, no way, or their friendship would be terminated. Kyle told him he was jealous and childish, and it was about time he forgot all the stupid old grudges. The look on Brendan's face told both of us that he was like Siegfried Sassoon: he swore by the Black Flag tattoo on his left bicep that he would never, ever forget. I weighed in heavily by telling him that he should be thinking of Dekkar, not himself, and if he was a real friend, he should support Dekkar in whatever it took to get well again. Brendan scowled at me for a moment, called me a hippie, then left the house, slamming every door in his vicinity on the way out. We could hear him on his way to the pub, punching and kicking the corrugated-iron fences along the back alley.

CHAPTER NINE

Cheap port and casual sex

I was on the Number 57 West Maribyrnong tram one day, winding through the back streets of North Melbourne on a rumour that someone or other had set up a screen printing shop somewhere along the tram line. The clothes were meant to be great, but the people I asked were keeping it a secret. Eyes glued to the shops as they cruised by, I didn't even notice Beckett until he had sat next to me and started talking about public transport all over the world.

'I think I like Gondolas the best,' he finally said in the kind of voice that many Melburnians slip on to appear cultured. I looked around at him and recognised him as one of Roman's old friends, from the halcyon days when I first came to Melbourne. All those faces; all those parties. He recognised me immediately and we started swapping Roman stories. He'd seen him a couple of months ago in Sydney, when he was doing something or other with the Dead Kennedys' tour. I'd spoken to Roman a couple of days ago on the phone, when I was visiting people who'd elected not to pay their phone bill.

'Seeing as we're almost family,' Beckett said, 'hows about you buy me lunch?'

Beckett wasn't exactly a handsome man. He looked exceedingly ordinary in fact. Short brown hair, beady little eyes, little round glasses. But after ten minutes with him in the Astoria Taxi Cab cafe, I was really liking him. He was the quickest person I'd met in ages. Everyone I knew was slow.

Beckett was his real name. He had a brother named Brecht and a sister named Joyce. His parents had been fifties bohemians: now they were both Labour Party officials. He lived in Caulfield with a mob of ex-punkers, most of whom worked on Saturdays at the racecourse. Beckett, however, had a real job as a computer technician. He asked me, 'So what do you do, Caitlin?'

'Oh,' I said, madly thinking of something to say which would sound impressive, 'I do clubs, drugs and other four letter words.'

When our food was ready – two hamburgers without the hamburger – we went outside and sat on Spencer Street, to watch the public and private transport go by. Beckett raved about the bus ride through the industrial wasteland to Footscray. I turned up my nose and told him I'd never been there and wasn't sure I wanted to. Next bus that came along, we were on it.

We rode buses through the western suburbs of Melbourne all day, ending up near the huge petrochemical plants in Altona. Beckett was taking photos of giant cranes and chemical storage units. I was hanging out for smack. We watched the sun go down under the Westgate bridge, and then Beckett said, 'Want to come to a party?' After four hours of heavy industry, I needed it.

Trains, buses and trams flashed before my eyes, and suddenly we were back in Carlton. Familiar territory. We'd spent all of our money on transport fares and greasy food and could only rustle up $5.64 between us for alcohol, so I walked into a tiny pub nestled between two housing commission towers, slapped the coinage down on the counter and said, 'I want something that's gonna suck the brains right out of my head.' It was an obliging pub, usually catering to the local derelicts, and the guy behind the counter didn't bat an eyelid. He produced two bottles of diabolical port, and didn't worry about the change.

Beckett reckoned that the only way to drink such a substance was sitting on a bus stop, out of a paper bag. So we positioned ourselves, twisted the brown paper around the bottles, opened them, then attempted to drink. Both initial mouthfuls were cast immediately on the footpath. I tried a second and managed to swallow. It burnt all the way down and made me shiver so much Beckett thought I was going into convulsions. The third caused less shaking. The fourth barely touched the sides.

The effect of cheap port was alarmingly similar to the effects of bad acid. By the time we rolled up to the house where the party was, everything was dark and slow and the noise was muffled. I was sure I was going to be sick at any moment. We walked into a tiny, claustrophobic house, and I had to run straight back outside to vomit. I saw a shining red Corvette parked under a streetlight, just asking for it. I was shameless.

'Caitlin!' a familiar voice said, 'you're shameless.'

Dekkar was standing in the doorway of the house, laughing at me. I wiped my mouth and laughed diabolically, and then emptied the rest of the port from my stomach. Dekkar laughed even more, then called into the house, 'Hey, everybody – ' I jumped across the footpath in an attempt to shut him up. But I misjudged badly, and we both went over, through the doorway, onto the floor, in the middle of the party room. It was an inauspicious beginning to a thoroughly debauched night.

Before I was even off the floor, I realised I had walked into something that I might regret in the morning. It was Shane's house, and this was Dekkar's moving in party. Brendan had done all but forbid Kyle and I to go, but I was there and so was she, in a black sequined dress, chatting up some guy who was undoubtedly a honey. I waved to her and then noticed Shane sitting on a cane couch, looking like he was having an intense kind of time with some woman who was also undoubtedly a honey. He'd seen me fall in the door, but looked like he was pretending he hadn't.

'Excuse me,' Dekkar's voice said, and I realised he was

underneath me, and the remains of my bottle of port were pouring over his brand new Iggy Pop T-shirt.

'That's okay,' I told him. 'He'd approve.'

I don't know what happened to me that night. I drank a wild mixture of beer, vodka, ouzo, champagne and then, when people saw me coming and hid their alcohol, the rest of the cheap port. Which I was handling all right – just – until Kyle passed me a joint and said, 'Here, have a bang of this number – ' My head started spinning like Linda Blair, and Kyle got me outside just before I let fly with the green spew. Then, my body just gave up.

I was unconscious for a while, and it felt pretty good, until a door seemed to open and a woman's voice screeched, 'Shane! That girl is in your bed!' I pried open my eyes and saw that honey of a girl standing in the doorway, silhouetted by red light. Another silhouette appeared – Shane's, by the hair and the height – and his voice said, 'Oh, that's all right, it's only Caitlin.' I closed my eyes again and thought, Kyle, I'll kill you for this. And then I went back to sleep, the only place I wasn't making an ass of myself.

When I crawled out in the middle of the night, still drunk, but not too drunk to know how I looked, it was all quiet. I found the bathroom, doused my head in a sink full of cold water, then fooled myself that I was sober and that fresh make-up might improve my state. From the window I could see it was still dark. That meant I could still attempt a dignified getaway, to cover for the rest of my ignominy.

'Ah!' Dekkar's voice said when I stepped into the lounge-room doorway. It was all dark, just one candle, and when my eyes adjusted, I saw half a dozen heads sitting amid a cloud of hash smoke. I went straight for Dekkar, who was slouched on the floor in a dark corner.

'Oh, Dekkar,' I said mournfully, and he laughed and put his arm around me, stoned and beaming health since his stint in the hospital, 'did you see what happened to that boy I came with?'

'Beckett? He saw you spewing in the garden and left. He was embarrassed.' Dekkar was cracking up. 'He apologised to Shane for bringing you.' The whole room burst into laughter at my expense. Even Shane, half hidden by shadows, suffered small convulsive giggles. This went on for a few minutes, until I realised that I was probably the most sober person in the room. Which wasn't saying much for the rest of them.

'All right, that's enough,' I said finally, 'someone give me a cigarette.'

'Here,' Shane said from across the room, and he crawled over to my side and sat next to me, a full pack of cigarettes in his hand. 'If you're sure Brendan won't mind.'

I took the cigarette and minced, 'Leave Brendan out of it.'

Everyone in the room said, 'Ooooh', like kids in the schoolyard waiting for a fight to erupt.

'All right,' Shane said, 'you want to let him dictate to you, that's your business.'

'Oh, shut up or I'll go vomit on your bed.'

He struck a match and an almost humorous expression. I dragged the flame through my cigarette, then expelled the smoke high up into the air. This was the kind of situation that could get me into trouble.

'I think I'd better go home,' I said out loud, and everyone in the room went, 'Aaawww', as if I'd pulled the plug on some kind of amusement. 'Dekkar, give me some money for a taxi.' He reached into his pocket and compliantly gave me a five dollar note, and Shane said, 'I'll call you a cab.' He got up and staggered into the next room. I had a swig of vodka from Dekkar's bottle then followed him.

I sat on the kitchen table and waited while he made a call, and then laughed when he said the taxi wouldn't be here till next July. He reckoned when he complained, they told him his best bet would be to get fucked. I'd never seen him so drunk before. Or so confident. Once I'd decided, it was a bit like taking candy from a baby. I said, 'Oh, well, we'd better have sex then.' He pretended to be reluctant. 'Yes, I suppose you're right.' We didn't talk after that.

Beckett called me a couple of days later, and we went out to see some bands. He told me I was the life of the party the other night, and he felt bad about just leaving me there, but he met up with an old girlfriend and with one thing and another, you know. I said yeah, I know. And we stood nodding knowingly for a while, until I asked, 'So how did it go?' He looked embarrassed and told me that he was so drunk he couldn't remember. It was that cheap port that did it: he should have thrown up like I did. Funny thing, though, he went round to Dekkar and Shane's place the next day to retrieve his glasses, which incidentally were broken, and Shane had suffered a similar fate. The two of them underwent a little male bonding as they tried to recall what they might have said and done, then decided what the hell, casual sex is casual sex. Did I get home all right? I smirked to myself, and told him that I had a bit of a wait for a taxi but, yes, I got home all right. 'Good,' he said, and then he turned back to watch the band.

CHAPTER TEN

Heroes

A couple of days before the New Year, with much unconscious apprehension about the upcoming 1984, a David
Bowie song repeating mercilessly in my head, and enduring
the first symptoms of withdrawal from heroin, I was
cruising down Brunswick Street, as one often does when
there's nothing else to do, trying to convince myself that
the sunshine was pleasant. It was hot, and heat was one
thing I didn't find pleasant any more. I stayed indoors,
in a sordid way revelling in the decadence of a household of heroin, depressed because my dole cheque was
late, and that Brendan had been hijacked by his parents
for a while. But even if he'd been here it wouldn't have
made any difference, because he was only interested in
friendship. I knew there was no chance, and that was
a good excuse to moon around Fitzroy with a scowl on
my face.

'"We could be heroes,"' I sang under my breath, self-
mocking, '"just for one day."'

Two days to a taste and Brendan, and I was just filling

in time. The kind of aimlessness that usually got me into trouble and kept the gossips and moralists in business.

'Hi! Cait!'

I looked up from my intense scrutiny of the footpath to set eyes on Dekkar and Shane. Dekkar was his usual bright and cheerful self, the new improved version since recovering from his smack withdrawal and intestinal tract problem. It was the same Dekkar who'd arrived from Sydney, ready and rearing to start a new life for himself. Shane just sort of hovered behind sunglasses and designer straggly hair, no trace of facial expression. Which was just as well, because if he'd been nice to me I would have been sick.

Dekkar tried to talk me into going to someone's place to smoke some hash. Smoking just didn't interest me these days at all. But that's not the sort of thing you say to a recent convert to a chemical-free way of life, for all you get is lectures. Well-meaning ones, especially from Dekkar, but when it comes to heroin, you can't tell anybody anything. So we were polite. After a flimsy excuse from me, we parted company. Shane hadn't spoken a word or even looked at me, as far as I could tell from my side of the sunglasses force field. That suited me fine.

I had gone about half a block when I heard footsteps close behind me, and I turned to see Shane. I didn't feel anything. It was as if he was a ghost, not even there. I don't know what his eyes were doing behind the sunglasses, but his voice quietly said, 'Can I buy you a drink?'

I should have turned and kept walking. That's what my head said. But my body – my *need* – got the better of me. I checked out his structure and decided, yes, he'd be good for it.

'Make it a taste and you're on.'

I regretted it the moment I said it. But while I knew Brendan would go insane if he knew I'd even spoken to Shane, all I could really think about was feeling better. And Shane knew the score.

'Okay. But we'll have to go back to my place.'

I nodded, bleeding from my morals like a stuck pig.

By daylight, the house was tiny. Tiny little rooms, all seeming to open on to each other. We wound our way across seagrass matting to the kitchen, and he put on an electric jug. 'I've only got some morphine,' he mumbled, slipping off the sunglasses to reveal bloodshot, stoned eyes, 'I don't use much any more.'

'Yeah,' I said, looking around so as to avoid his eyes, but taking in nothing, 'so I hear.'

He left the room and then came back with a small cardboard box of Morphine vials. About six or seven of them altogether: a junkie's paradise. And, hell, my stomach was churning like the first time I fell in love. I really had to work to contain my excitement. For a moment I thought he was going to ask me something, like how I was, or express some concern about me. Or – horror – mention the night of the party. But he didn't, and I was glad. He gave me the whole box without a word, and I accepted in matching silence. As I was leaving, I forced myself to say, 'See you.' But I wasn't looking at him, and he probably wasn't looking at me, and his reply, 'Yeah, see you,' swam away with the Rathdowne Street traffic.

Kyle was there when I got home. She didn't ask where the vials came from, and I didn't tell her. We spent the next twelve hours in a sea of bliss on her waterbed, unconcerned with men or money or anything but whatever was on her tiny television. Eventually, we started talking about money and men and everything. Men, mostly. She told me Big Danny Herlihy, a drug-addled taxi driver who was a constant source of information, saw me coming out of Shane Brophy's place this afternoon. As far as she was concerned, of course, I was there to see Dekkar: but even so, perhaps it was time for the two of us to start working on Brendan. His macho feud was alienating people left right and centre. It wasn't fair on innocent bystanders – meaning herself – or the people involved – meaning myself. I told her I reckoned we were all innocent bystanders. Especially me. Okay, she said, it was up to us.

And then she closed her eyes and nodded off again. Eyes closed myself, I waited for a while to hear her master plan, then figured she'd gone to sleep. It was after all, 3 AM. I rolled out of the bed carefully, which is almost impossible on a waterbed, then went down to my room and tried to figure out how it all became so complicated.

I wasn't always a coward, a procrastinator extraordinaire. Late at night – it's always late at night when I think about Cal – I can remember the adrenalin rush when we decided to go ahead with the plant harvest in the absence of our other partners. We'd forward Dorland and Jordan's shares to them, once we knew where they were. That was the plan.

Of course an adrenalin rush denotes fear or fright, but I didn't figure that at the time. Early evening, sometime in January, we pulled up the plants and rested them in pillows of silicone gel. I was obsessed by the gentle flickering in Cal's eyes. The flickering kept up for a week, as we checked on the plants, and dried out the bags of gel that absorbed the fragrant moisture. The flickering matched the torpedoes in my stomach, the obsession in my head.

One week night, Cal turned up in a car he said he'd borrowed from Old Staff. I believed him, of course. I had little to no experience with untruths. We laid the harvest – seven and a half pounds – out in the boot, covered it with a travel rug and implements of sensible motoring. It would take four and a half hours to get to Lismore.

Twenty minutes down the road to the coast, Cal pulled over to the side of the road with the vaguest suggestion of a smoke. I was nervous with the load in the boot and what amounted to my first night out with Cal. He went to the boot while I drenched my lungs with eucalypt vapour.

'Close your eyes,' Cal's voice told me from somewhere in the darkness and mosquitoes, 'I've got a surprise for you.'

I closed my eyes: sixteen and brave and in love.

The surprise was a belt with the car's jack across the back of my head.

I opened my eyes: two weeks older and in hospital.

With the memory came the pain in the back of my head. Shit, I didn't need Freudian analysis to tell me I equate love with pain. It's one thing to dabble in self-analysis: behaviour modification is another thing altogether. A slow creep up to Kyle's room for another vial – to annul the pain – and the clock in the corner told me it was 4.45. I wanted the dawn to see me as something other than a coward. A quick hit instilled the bravery I needed.

Huddled on the first floor landing, I dialled the number to clear my conscience. Five in the morning is a hell of a time to do it, but I couldn't sleep. My room's cavernous proportions were oppressive: the ghosts swimming around whispered words I should have said. The tone on the phone denoted ringing: a click denoted arrival at goal. Shane's sleepy cold voice denoted connection.

'Yeah?'

'It's Caitlin.' As an afterthought, I added, 'Steele.'

He muttered, 'I only known one Caitlin,' as if it was a curse.

'I'm sorry to ring so late,' I told him, directed by the voices of the ghosts of my room, 'but there's something I have to say. I'm sorry about what happened this afternoon. There is no excusing it: I was rude and cold, and felt guilty because of what Brendan might think. I just want you to know that it won't happen again. He's not going to dictate to me, and he's not going to bag you out any more. That's all, really.'

There was a long pause. Then the sound of some kind of movement, like he was moving in bed, and he said, 'You want to come round?'

It was tempting. I could picture him, lying in bed. But there was something to take care of first.

'Yeah, but I can't. Not till I sort this problem out.'

Another pause, accompanied by a comfortable sigh. 'Okay. Whenever.' It was the comfort in the sigh that confirmed I'd done the right thing.

Doing the right thing was not as easy as it should have been. When Brendan walked in the door, full of horror stories about going away for two days with his family, how he'd NEVER do it again, and shit he needed some hard drugs, I couldn't spin him out straight away. So I suggested a drink at the Standard, then stood on Kyle's toes so she'd take the hint.

Eyes watering, she said, 'Uh, no, big night tonight. I have to go to see Jeremy.' Jeremy was the local trendy hairdresser, and he worshipped Kyle – he always did her hair for nothing. The two of them together – gossipmonger heaven.

'Your shout,' Brendan said two and a half hours later, when for one reason or another I still hadn't summoned the courage. Then it was forced upon me. A strange click of fate. Shane walked into the lounge, with Dekkar and Beckett. Brendan saw them the same time I did, and turned around with his mouth open. I put my hand over it and said, 'Before you say anything, let me tell you something. If you so much as LOOK at Shane, or say one detrimental thing, I'm going to slap your face and never speak to you again. I mean it. I think you're wonderful, but I can't take this shit any more. Please don't disappoint me.'

I watched Shane and the others hot-tail it through to the front bar, out of our vision, and then took my hand away from Brendan's mouth. He stared at me for a moment, looking decidedly humble.

'I didn't know you felt this deeply about him.'

His tone could have been calculating. I decided to read it as quietly honest. I said, 'I feel – DEEPLY, as you put it – about a lot of people. And you're at the top of the list, arsehole.'

'Prove it. Buy me a drink.'

Loosened by a double vodka and orange, courtesy my dole cheque, Brendan admitted that he knew he had a problem with all this, but he couldn't help it. He wanted to punish Shane for something that happened in the past.

Jealousy – yes, he knew the word – and sexual insecurity. I was surprised by his candour. A young man exposing even a glimpse of his sexuality was a rare sight, even in supposedly liberated times.

'Oh, I couldn't imagine sexual insecurity being much of a problem,' I told him, swigging the last of my hard drink, 'big strapping boy like you.' Brendan grinned, as he always did when I used cliches and quaint terms. I leant forward and said, 'Of course, I can only speculate – ' And then he leant forward and kissed me.

It was wonderful. I'd waited for another kiss since the first day we met. In those days, he was running away from Deidre, his jealous monster. On that day, when the kiss ended, his vision and broad smile turned in the direction of the counter. And, through there, to the front bar. I glanced around and saw Shane, Dekkar and Beckett, all leaning on the bar, looking at us. It didn't take a computer to figure out that Brendan's so-called honesty was an excuse to sink the knife in. I said, 'Bastard,' under my breath, and not much else.

Two drinks and an ashtray over Brendan's head later, I was running down the side lane towards Brunswick Street fighting back tears of anger and humiliation.

Brendan called, 'Caitlin!' and he came into sight, cigarette butts stuck in his mohawk.

I knocked them out with a clout across his head and screamed, 'I hate you!'

He hit me back and screamed, 'Well, I hate you too!'

I was stunned, took a step back and, after some contemplation, said, 'Well, that's all right then.'

And it was as all right as it was ever going to be. We traded minor apologies that neither of us meant, locked into our serious symbiosis. Jealousy, anger, hate, it didn't matter much. At the end of the day, or the beginning of the hangover, we needed each other.

'So,' Brendan said eventually, ignoring the small crowd that had gathered during our slapping display, 'you still want to go and see Nick Cave tonight?'

I must have laughed hysterically. 'Why not? We'll all go fucking neurotic together.'

Brendan laughed hysterically too, though probably at something else. And we started walking again, past the op shops and the greasy cafes, and down through the housing commission flats. This took considerable bravery, the way we were dressed. By the time we'd reached Gertrude Street, I didn't care about being a coward any more. Just walking along with Brendan was enough.

CHAPTER ELEVEN

Big Brother is not watching

31 December 1983. Nearly eleven. All of us supposedly on our way to the Nick Cave gig at the Ballroom, until the Temptation got us. 'It's all these Nick Cave records' was a lousy excuse, but who cared? Brendan went to score. Kyle and I made ourselves up in the kitchen. Marcie had locked herself in the bathroom again. Kyle said, 'One day, she'll OD in there.' She gave a positively wicked smile. No one cared about Marcie any more. Not since Dominic saw her riding in a cop car. We were tolerant people, but we could not tolerate a grass.

'She probably gets good dope off the cops, though,' Kyle added, pretending not to be edgy about Brendan's expedition. 'Although you get some damn fine morph, too. So where did that come from? As if I need to ask.'

She had that beautiful smile on her face, so I could never get too annoyed. Yeah, she knew where I'd got it from, and suspected I'd done a hell of a lot to get it.

'He gave it to me, that's all.'

The clock was inching towards midnight. There was a

strong possibility that Brendan would be all over town tonight. Even dealers went to New Year's Eve parties. I tried to convince myself that it wouldn't matter if we didn't get on.

'Really, it doesn't matter to me if we score or not.'

Kyle pointed out that I said that every time we were waiting, but as soon as I heard the car, I was boiling water and collecting spoons and filters like sped-up film. That was the main problem with smack, as far as I could see. You're always saying, 'I've got it under control, I can handle it.' Always strong, self-centred thoughts, until the sound of the car outside –

1 January 1984. 12.06 AM. I staggered to my feet and methodically rinsed out my fit. The rush took hold of me like a liquid vice. Brendan smiled, knowing a good taste when he saw one. I headed outside, passing Dekkar in the kitchen. He'd hitched a lift from St Kilda with Brendan, on his way to a party in Carlton. My condition did not seem to worry him too much. He smiled and said, 'Happy New Year.'

I floated on out to the back yard. When I had emptied my stomach, I looked up at the sky. It was clear, perfect, dotted with beautiful stars. It was like 1984 was never going to happen.

Louie Louie/we gotta go –

The music was blaring, melting down the walls, the graffiti slipping away. I half skanked into the kitchen, cool and confident and myself again, because I'd sussed out that the only time I really enjoyed smack was when I had a little habit going.

The clock said 12.13 AM. Thirteen minutes into 1984. I knew that something bad was going to happen. And it wasn't just that Brendan's Black Flag record was scratched. Though that was disastrous enough. My body began to heave.

Kyle was standing in the hallway, looking into the lounge-room, sobbing uncontrollably. Something very serious. I knew it, but didn't want to know. Yeah, tuning out always helped. Thinking, listening.

I heard Dekkar yelling, 'Get an ambulance!' and saw Kyle darting off. I felt like I was floating into the lounge-room, until I fell against the record player.

Force that shit right through my head/if I don't get out/I'm gonna be dead.

Brendan was ODing. Dekkar was doing CPR. Brendan's face was framed by the cheap Persian rug, a small smile on his lips, his eyes slightly open. I grabbed his arm and shook it, saying, 'Wake up you arsehole. Don't you spoil my new year!' But his arm was completely limp. No resistance.

'Why aren't you fucking breathing?' Dekkar screamed, pushing hard and deep into Brendan's sternum. 'You SHOULD be breathing.'

His hand was warm, but without a pulse.

Louie Louie/we gotta go –

I knelt beside him and held his wrist and watched Dekkar and it went forever. Till Kyle came in, hugging me. Till the ambulance people came, and pushed back all the furniture, and milled all over Brendan. I listened to their words with a mixture of perfect clarity and abject horror. They were still fighting, but the battle was over. Brendan's body was empty. He was gone. I ran out into the back yard and screamed, until all the breath was out of my lungs. It was an insane appeal.

Even the stars were gone.

CHAPTER TWELVE

Here we go, here we go, here we go

I didn't think I was going to make it past the first hour, let alone the first week. Most of it was spent staring down the toilet, during some illness or other. A big, twisting tunnel. Brendan was never there.

People were very supportive. They kept us in smoke and drink and pills. Kyle and I spent the whole time in her room, since Brendan's parents turned up and completely stripped his. It infuriated us until we realised that they had their own difficulties. They weren't A-Grade parents, and they were probably going through a major guilt crisis. We were understanding enough when we'd dropped a few Serapax. Like sea sponges.

The funeral was pretty bleak. Searing heat out at the Springvale Crematorium, there was a divisive line between Brendan's relatives and his friends, like two feuding families. In the middle, in a red wood coffin on a roller trolley was Brendan. Well, I supposed it was Brendan. His family wouldn't let us see him.

The service started with a man of the cloth saying a

prayer. This, and the pills I had taken earlier, and the heat, made me feel very sick. I wanted to stand up and scream, 'He hated this!' but I feared I would laugh or cry or vomit on the priest. So I clenched my fists. His parents were completely stiff. Some uncle got up and talked about when Brendan was a boy. And then, right when they appeared to be attempting 'The Lord's my Shepherd', Kyle turned to me and said, 'Puke City!' I threw up.

It certainly saved the whole event from being a complete disaster, although I didn't get a chance to sit around and enjoy the spectacle. Dekkar whisked me outside to some toilets, and we both cracked up laughing, and crying. Kyle reckoned that the whole place erupted: Brendan's friends were laughing, his family was outraged. Dominic and Mad Lenny – either grief-mad or shickered, or both – couldn't stop laughing. They pretended they were crying, but everyone knew. The minister ignored them and finalised the grim little service, and then, as the coffin began to slide away through a curtain, they started chanting, 'Here we go, here we go, here we go – ' The Suits, all the size of mountains, tried to escort them out, and there was a scuffle. Dominic and Mad Lenny spent the rest of the day in the local lock-up. The rest of us went home and imbibed ourselves to oblivion. It was the only thing we were good at.

CHAPTER THIRTEEN

One month in Sydney without a dole cheque

It had been two days since Brendan went up in smoke. They felt like an eternity. I started to lose control. When a loud-mouthed politically correct anarchist named Mac Ronald dropped in, Kyle explained to him about Brendan. Mac Ronald looked around and said, 'Well, that's the risk you people take, isn't it?'

I was sitting there, scraping tar from the water bong pipe with a hopelessly oversized carving knife. Next thing I knew, I had slapped Mac Ronald's jibbering mouth and was waving the knife against his throat, hissing, 'Let's play slash the anarchist!' Dekkar jumped up and down on the couch, saying 'Yes, let's!' Mac Ronald never came back. I laughed and laughed.

I heard Kyle on the phone to someone, saying she was worried I was going crazy. I don't know who she was talking to. Could have been the Time Man.

Two hours later, Shane came around. He wouldn't step in the front door.

'Well, what do you want?' I said stiffly. I knew he

wouldn't come around without a good reason. And I doubted Kyle would be silly enough to bring him over to discuss me.

'Your help.'

I couldn't believe my ears. No one asked for my help. Or advice. Probably because I was always issuing it, freely and profusely. He said Roman was arriving back tomorrow morning, and he didn't know about Brendan yet.

'I don't want him to find out over the phone, or on the grapevine.'

What he was asking became clear.

Half an hour later, I was in the car with him heading along Sydney Road, Coburg. His driving hadn't improved since the night we saw 'Eraserhead', but I was too doped to notice. Going to Sydney would be a diversion. Anything to get through the day. I dropped more Serapax and lost consciousness before the end of the tram line.

I woke up in a traffic jam on Parramatta Road. I looked around calmly for a moment, and then realised I was in Sydney. That was the thing with pills. Memory loss. Shane was driving pretty damn dangerously, hidden behind dark glasses so I couldn't see how tired he looked. I closed my eyes again, and we were at the airport. And then Roman was there. He looked fantastic. More handsome then ever, like some kind of rock star. People's heads turned when they saw him, as if he was someone they should recognise.

'Shane!' he exclaimed, hugging his old mate with laughs of surprise, 'and Caitlin! What are you two doing here?'

I felt so sick I was sure I was going to lose it. Roman saw me go green and he looked to Shane. Shane looked to me, sending me an 'I need you now!' message. I took a deep breath. Roman was already pale. He fumbled blindly for a cigarette.

'Brendan,' I said, taking hold of his arm. His eyes were clear and wide and panicked.

'What?' he said, and I lived through it again, there in the international terminal. I tried very hard to speak without crying.

'He's dead.'

Roman looked at us both, and then tried to light a cigarette. His lips were trembling so much, he had no hope. The cigarette just bounced around in their air, until it fell when he yelled out, 'No!'

We spent the afternoon going from one bar to the next, gradually working our way across Sydney's inner suburban landscape until we arrived at something resembling dinner time in Kings Cross. Shane and Roman were walking disaster areas, and I was their minder. Quite a role reversal for me. I shepherded them into what had all the appearances of being a clean establishment. As soon as the food arrived – Nachos, of all things – Roman threw up all over the table. He was so clean cut and perfectly poised that the waiter thought he was genuinely ill. Presently a taxi came. Roman was beyond conversation. Shane couldn't remember where Roman lived. I went back into the cafe, and my hunch was right. The waiter was a friend. He wrote down Roman's address, and said he'd come round when his shift finished.

It was only a couple of blocks to the half-dilapidated terrace down the bitumen cul-de-sac. Many of the houses – all identical terraces – sported optimistic baby gums in their front yards. Right under the power lines. What hope for the young?

'Oi,' I said, jabbing Shane in the ribs when I'd paid the fare, 'wake up, Bucko, I need your help with laughing boy.'

True, Roman was gurgling to himself in some kind of infantile regression, his black shirt dotted with foul-smelling vomit. Shane shook his head and mumbled, 'I didn't think you wanted me for my body.' And he grudgingly helped me get Roman out to the street, up the path and to the front door. We looked in his pockets for keys, but no luck. Shane said we'd have to break in. He was serious, but too drunk to do much.

We left Roman lying face-down on his front doorstep and dodged hundreds of Heineken empties down the side path to get to the back of the house. Shane reckoned the bathroom window was a cinch, but it involved one of us climbing up on the laundry roof first.

'You sure know how to show a girl a good time,' I said, as he cupped his hands to provide me with a leg-up.

'You wouldn't know a good time if it chainsawed your ovaries.'

I didn't let him see the pleasure in my eyes. I stepped up on his hand and took hold of the laundry roof's guttering.

It had been raining. The guttering hadn't been cleared for a long time. A huge splash of cold, dirty water hit Shane on the top of the head, and soaked him through. I sat above him on the laundry roof and laughed and laughed. A really clear laugh, without supernatural reproach. Shane shook himself like a dog just out of a bath, cursed me to hide his own amusement, then went around to the front of the house.

The house was pitch black inside, and there wasn't a standard light switch to be found. I made my way through the bathroom, down a hallway, and only discovered the stairs when I had tumbled half way down. My steady drinking meant I rolled and bounced: I came to rest in a downstairs hallway, red light filtering through stained-glass windows around the front door.

'You took your time,' Shane snapped when I opened the door. He took hold of one of Roman's arms, dragging him onto the front door step.

'I fell down the stairs,' I told him, rubbing a sore shoulder.

'Oh, really?' he said with genuine care in his voice, dropping Roman smack on the floor and touching my sore shoulder with no hesitation, 'are you okay?' I nodded. The human touch felt good. 'Just your shoulder?'

I was sober enough to know that he was too drunk to know what he was doing. But the thought of stopping him didn't enter my mind. I told him my ribs were sore. He caressed them, slipping his hand under my T-shirt. My right hip, I said, and he caressed them both. I kissed him: we turned into different people. We didn't make it to a bedroom. Didn't make it past the bottom of the staircase.

When I came, something happened that I hadn't counted on. The truth rose up like a machete, cutting me to pieces. I howled.

Shane pulled away and stared at me as if he suddenly remembered who I was. Confused, he didn't seem to know what I was doing there, let alone why I was crying. I covered my face with my hands, shattered and humiliated. When I looked out again, he was gone, and Roman was still lying face-down on the front doorstep where he'd left him.

When I woke up, it was night time and Roman was okay. He was making cappuccinos down in the kitchen for half-a-dozen passers-by who'd heard he was back in town. Off-handedly explaining that Shane was on his way back to Melbourne, he introduced me to people as his old friend Caitlin who had come to stay for a while. That was just the beginning.

Activity, and plenty of it. Parties, introductions, drink, drugs, loud music, dancing, shopping. Roman even got me on a ferry. I had no money, and even less inclination to rustle some up, so he paid for me everywhere I went. Which, he said, was not a problem. What he could not charge to his company he would bill me for with interest at some time when I least expected it. He was intensely caring, making up for everything. Making up for Brendan, when we both knew nothing could. So we kidded each other we were helping each other out. Which we were, in the waking hours at least. At night, or early morning, to be precise, we went into separate rooms, into separate horrors. His were of a teenage friend. Mine were of my best friend. As the days passed, each one to our massive relief that it was actually over, the horror became more subtle. It wasn't at the forefront of my thoughts all the time. Sometimes I would even forget. Then it would hit me in a massive wave. He's gone. He's dead. I'm never going to see him again. Never going to talk to him again. The waves subsided into a slow, gradual depression. I slept as much as I could, trying to dream of Brendan. But if I did dream, I didn't remember. Whatever was going on in the other world was out of my grasp. And what was in my grasp, while being aesthetically pleasing, was never satisfying. I went through the routines: did what was absolutely necessary. But then I'd find that I'd been staring at a blank wall for an hour. Food was abhorrent. Alcohol was vital. Life was just hovering. I knew it was there, somewhere.

But I came to realise I would get back into it, one day. I came to realise I would survive. Some nights I stared through the window across the rooftops and called to Brendan. Up there with the stars. Tell me what it's like. Talk to me again. Give me a sign. What's it like? What's it like? Did you hear Louie Louie when you went out? Did you hear the music I played for you? Do you miss your body? What's it like? What's it like? Screaming in my sleep, What's it like?

He never answered. That's the thing about death. I'd just have to wait and see.

CHAPTER FOURTEEN

The road and the soup

Blistering hot afternoon. Approaching Melbourne down the Hume Highway, old punk tapes blaring until my brain shook, I wailed at Roman, 'I'm going to explode, or melt, or splatter like water on hot oil.' I was boiling over there on the passenger side while Roman, on the other side of some intangible air coolant barrier, cruised along behind the wheel, looking like an ad from 'The Face'. Not a bead of sweat. Not a millilitre of melted hair gel. Unashamedly singing in a woefully flat voice, '"I'm an orgasm addict, I'm always at it."' Straight through Truck City.

He told me a funny story about a time when he and Brendan and Caroline and Shane stopped there, at that roadhouse, to get cigarettes. A Tom Jones song was on the radio. He and Brendan started dancing: Caroline screamed and ripped off her underpants. Shane told them they were being disgusting and rushed them away, without paying for four packs of cigarettes. With a giggle Roman said, 'Caroline lost her underpants, but then she was always doing that.'

I asked him if he was very upset when she died. He watched Truck City disappear through the rear-vision mirror then told me that at the time he thought he was very upset. But it was nothing compared to losing Brendan. And that was nothing to losing his grandmother. Every one, he supposed, was different. And he'd done quite enough sampling for the time being, so could I please make sure I didn't up and die? We were heading into Melbourne. I said I'd give it my best shot. And I certainly wouldn't lose my underpants. Ha, I thought to myself, I should be so lucky. And then I thought that life really was beginning to return to normal.

Straight to my place. On the doorstep, still glaze-eyed from endless hours, endless motion from one metropolis to another, we passed the time enthusing about what was in store. Roman was extending his business to Melbourne: he was going to set up a record shop. I was going to run it. As soon as profits allowed, Kyle would be employed. Get us off the dole: keep us out of trouble. Shane would do the figures. Roman said he was very good with abstractions. A world of possibilities was unfolding before me, until I opened the door of the house as Roman darted off, calling to the whole neighbourhood, 'Gonna check out those drug fiends over in Carlton. Give me a ring at Shane's when you're ready.' He blended into the traffic and cars and heat, and I was there on my own doorstep. It didn't feel like my door. It didn't feel like my home. I didn't feel like me.

The smell was obvious, even from the front door. Old stinking garbage going off in the heat. A pile of mail was stuck between the door and the old, torn carpet. No-one had been around for a few days. Stepping past it, I unlocked the padlock Kyle had put on my door with the key she'd sent, dumping my worn-out overnight bag in the doorway. The room was cool. It always amazed me how this room could be so cold in such a swelter.

Down in the kitchen, psychedelic mould was growing on a host of cups and plates. There was the smell of rotting food, and that peculiar odour that always hovered in our kitchen – leaking gas from the fridge, someone reckoned. Permeating it all was a new, more pungent, mysterious smell.

I put on music in the hope that my ears might take on some of the nasal work. Electronic dance music buzzed through the house. It didn't cover the smell, but it did rouse a new neighbour. An angry Mediterranean man, standing over the patched-up fence that Sly used to climb through, shouted, 'Turn that down!' I feigned deafness.

Kyle's door was bolted, like mine. Dominic's was bolted too. Brendan's was open, cavernous, empty. Old Blutak marks on the paint and the smell of rotting stout – and that other smell. It was so strong it stopped me getting maudlin about Brendan.

On the telephone landing, it was putrid. Dominic's door was a couple of feet away. Along the hallway, towards

Marcie's room, it was stronger and stronger. I took off an excess shirt and wrapped it around my breathing apparatus, still half crazy from the road and not in complete control. There was no light down Marcie's end of the hallway. By the time I got to her door, it was dark and completely rancid. The door seemed to locked from inside. Confident I was alone, and detached from any sense of responsibility, I kicked the door in.

The smell ballooned out like one of Mad Lenny's right hooks.

Something was on the floor.

Gasping, I ran down to the telephone landing for fresher air, but the stench followed me like a horde of demons. I looked at the phone, then at myself in the mirror. My skin didn't look like that.

Back in Marcie's doorway, I knew what it was. Human – or it had been. I couldn't look at it for long without wanting to be sick. There were blowflies and maggots and a bluey red figure housing the colony. The hair was long and thin and turquoise. Beside what might have been an arm was a fit and the works. That's how I knew it was Marcie. I closed my eyes and my head told my heart that I should be crying. But I wasn't. It would take a lot to make me cry these days.

I felt barren. Devoid of emotion, the only thought of substance was that I was glad Brendan was cremated: glad his body didn't decompose like this. Stinking, fetid, abomin-able. Typical of Marcie: a big dramatic mess for someone else to clean up.

Seven tries later, I connected with Shane's number. That's where Roman was: that's where I hoped to hell Kyle was. After three rings, when I was sure Roman had hijacked them all for cappuccinos and cakes – I almost gagged at the thought of those fruit tarts with gelatin on top – the phone clicked on and there was a thump and a long silence. I was breathing so fast I could hardly talk.

'Who's that? Who's that?' I asked, and then a recorded voice came on, Shane saying, 'Congratulations: you have failed to connect.' I slammed down the telephone, furious, and tried to locate Kyle, or Dominic, or anyone.

In the end, I gave up and sat with Marcie for a while. Not *with* her – I opened her window and sat in the sill – but close enough. There seemed little hurry. She wasn't going anywhere.

I was sitting with Marcie, but mostly I was sitting with myself. With my mother, possibly my father, Brendan. Join-ing them would be a cinch. Just let go of the window. See what the other side is like. See if there's clubs: go and get drunk with Brendan and Marcie. I wondered if Brendan would still be unattainable: I wondered if Marcie would still be so stupid.

The back gate creaked. The corrugated iron always

crashed as it came open. Marcie's room, at the back of the house, was virtually on the lane. The window was above the gate. I saw Shane long before he saw me.

'Hi!' I called from Marcie's window. Closing the gate, he looked around and then up and then at me, into the sun. Squinting, pained by direct skin contact with solar rays, it was obvious he wasn't feeling good.

'Roman said you'd be here,' he called up.

'The place is a dump,' I said back. I was shaking and sick in the stomach, but I could tell by my voice that I could cover it. I don't know why I was even trying.

'I know,' he said, taking a few steps towards the kitchen door. 'The smell is appalling. What are you doing up there?' He opened the door then stood still, waiting for some kind of response. I could have told him then, braced him, prepared him for the ghastly mess. I could have, right then. But I didn't.

'Come and see!' was what I told him. 'And can you pick up my handbag from the stairs on the way up?' He was already in the house. 'I want my camera,' I finished, to myself.

Shane stared at Marcie for a good ten minutes. I took polaroids and watched them develop, then laid them out along the windowsill. There was no wind. There was no air. When I was satisfied, I wrapped them up, put them in my bag and said to myself, That'll do for you. Shane was still frozen at the door, arm over his mouth and nose, in deep contemplation of the soup on the floor.

'So,' he said finally, distinctly muffled, 'how was Sydney?'

'Not too bad,' I told him, fighting to keep the shake from my voice, 'though I'd kill for a smoke.'

He nodded from behind the limb. 'That can be arranged.'

I did up the camera and put it in my bag. 'Good. Looks like a call to the authorities is going to be inevitable.'

'Better you than me.'

I nodded my head. The action caused minute air movement: more stench. 'If you see them, tell the others to lie low and keep their mouths shut.'

Nodding, he took the arm away from his face and braved it. I guess he worked out it wasn't so bad, when you got used to it. His lips were curling a little. Yeah, he had a cold heart. Just like me. He said, 'Anything else, Guv?'

'Yeah. Arrange that smoke.'

'I've got some blond hash I've been keeping for a special occasion.'

I grinned, with great effort, and glanced at Marcie. No-one had mentioned drugs in her presence for a long time. There was always the chance she'd raid your room, or tell her police mates.

'Well, break it out, Bucko.'

We smiled agreeably at each other, and then he left the way he'd come. I watched him go through the kitchen door and slink across the hot cobblestones. Part of me wanted to scream, Don't go: beam me up, out of this! But the stronger part knew I'd got this far without spinning out. If I could just handle the cops, then I knew I could handle anything. Nothing could threaten me any more.

The police were there within four minutes of the call. I was counting, sitting on the front doorstep. A couple of young constables – younger than me – got out of their car. I watched them approach and thought wickedly, Ah, this'll make your day.

'Okay, so what's the problem?' the guy said. I suppose he'd mainly done alcoholic domestics in the commission flats.

'Cop that smell?' I said, my voice weak from poisoned lungs, a deliberate monotone. The pair of them stepped into the doorway and looked at each other. Silently dealing on who was going in, the female officer shrugged and must have realised that affirmative action was going to rule. I took her up the stairs, lame-brained explaining I'd just got back from a month in Sydney, and I had no idea where anyone was. The second constable walked behind us, saying, 'Didn't we come here on an overdose death a while ago?' I thought about saying, Yes: we live a wild and crazy life, but decided against it.

The looks on their faces when they stepped into Marcie's room were enough. It was my revenge on all the cops who'd hassled me, beaten up my friends, and made life so difficult and paranoid. It was their initiation into real life. And then some. They turned to each other and then Dale, Constable Care, ran outside to be sick. It was a damn long hallway, so he had to be quick.

CHAPTER FIFTEEN

Cool

The city was melting. But I was cool. I sat on the steps and watched a parade of uniforms and bad suits go up and down the stairs. Then one of them stopped, introduced himself as Detective Sergeant Moon, and took me outside. We sat on his car bonnet and smoked cigarettes.

Doing an airhead routine to mask my complete lack of emotion, I convinced DS Moon that I'd stumbled home from Sydney, noticed the smell, gone upstairs, discovered Marcie, opened the window, then called them.

'You'll have to come down to the station to make a statement,' he said. Then he took another look at my face and added, 'Tomorrow will do.'

The stretcher-bearers wore masks as they carried Marcie to the ambulance. I seemed to be the only one not thoroughly sickened. What would her parents think?

In a crazy gesture, I offered to identify the body. This would save Marcie's parents, both cholesterol-ridden meat eaters from Warrnambool, risking heart attacks. A couple of phone calls, and we were on our way to the morgue.

On her bedroom floor, Marcie had been a human shape. At the morgue, she was merely remains. She had literally fallen apart when they tried to move her: spilt out all over the floor, I supposed. As I looked at what was left, all I could think about was whether the wretched body juices would leak down to the kitchen. Her turquoise hair was brown now, matted with the liquid.

Moon gave me a lift back to Fitzroy from the morgue, beginning to sniff for information. I made sure he could see that my arms were clean as I told him all about the traffic chaos in Sydney. If he was still interested after that, he kept it to himself.

He dropped me off at the corner of Brunswick and Gertrude. I watched the police car drive away, watched the people watching me, then started walking. Out of habit, I wandered into the op shops along Brunswick Street. Suddenly I was standing in deepest Fitzroy. It felt like one giant morgue.

Dominic and Mad Lenny came stumbling out of a shoe shop. They were loaded, yelling loud, Nazi punk boys on their cheque day worst behaviour. Dominic, at least a foot taller than me, said down his nose, 'You back from Sydney, eh? You seen Marcie?'

I almost did a flip right there outside the Black Cat cafe.

'Uh, yeah,' I said, vocal chords still poisoned. 'You?'

He shook his head, splattered a laugh and said, 'Bitch

owes me two hundred bucks.'

I smiled at Dominic, wished him luck, then, with a quick sharp jab to Mad Lenny's ribs, which I disguised as an accident, I was on my way. Feeling cooler and more together with every step, I didn't notice if I was sweating or getting sunburnt. By the time I got to Johnston Street, I'd said hello to half-a-dozen people I knew without making any reference to bodily decomposition. At the traffic lights I started to feel faint, more from lack of nutrition and the heat than any kind of shock. I put my hand up to shield the sun from my eyes and a taxi stopped.

Once inside Shane's lounge-room, which was virtually on Rathdowne Street, I realised that I stank of dead meat. This was obvious by the look on the face of the girl who let me in. She was young and very pretty, hand on the front door like some kind of style enforcer.

Ignoring the fact that I smelt bad, I tried to be friendly. 'I'm here to see Shane,' I told her.

She gave me a patronising smile and said, 'Join the queue.'

The one thing I hated more than being patronised was being patronised by someone I didn't know. This girl looked amiable enough, the kind that spring up from month to month around the band scene, then start hanging around the perceived cool people as some kind of social stratagem. Looking strange and smelling bad, I didn't match the stringent Cool People rules.

'Listen, shithead' – her eyes sharpened and her nose flared up – 'you don't know the day I've had. Now get out of my fucking way!' I was standing right up close, so she could get a good lungful. When my hand threatened to touch her, she jumped right away. There was a weird kind of joy in conscious intimidation. You could get a taste for it.

The lounge-room was crawling with strangers. They were all young and very fashion conscious, walking hair-dos with meticulously ripped clothes to reveal that tiny skull tattoo on the left shoulder blade. Over the thrash din, they didn't notice me, but they sure did notice the smell. I wondered what Shane was doing allowing all these apprentice punk rockers into his house, as I emitted fumes across the room, through the doorway, to the dining room. There I saw familiar faces. This must be the style sanctum. The inner circle of this tiny scene. Roman was holding court like a king. Kyle was chief consort and translator. Dekkar paraded around like a court jester, half a dozen skate punks worshipping his every move.

I waved across to Roman and called out, 'Where's Shane?'

He waved back and yelled, 'Look, everyone, it's Caitlin!'

It's not that I was very popular. I had a big mouth and I used it. I didn't sleep around very much, so many of the men I knew were intimidated. I didn't dress particularly well, or put much effort into my hair. I wasn't easily defined as a punk, or a trendy, or anything else, for that matter.

Yet, I had to endure a rousing reception of people saying, 'Yo Caitlin!' and cheering whoops and making out like I was some kind of homecoming queen. I'd only been away for a month. Perhaps they'd forgotten who I was.

'Where's Shane?' I asked Beckett, who was already quizzing me on my perceptions of the Sydney public transport system. He pointed towards the bathroom, a curious expression, like 'What is that smell?' sweeping behind his specs.

To get to the bathroom, I had to squeeze through a kitchen full of violated Danish pastries and empty cask wine bladders. Forcing myself to nod, I got through without getting caught. When I was at the bathroom door, I heard Kyle cry out, 'Phew, what's that smell?' And then they all looked at Dekkar, who was never a great one for hygiene. They didn't notice me leave.

The sun blazed the trail from Carlton to Fitzroy with me. I was on automatic now, thinking, I must go home. I have to go home. Only the home I wanted to go to was much further than George Street, Fitzroy. I found a public phone that worked, but James didn't answer. He was probably down at the dam, or tending to his dope crop, or doing something else that didn't involve police and coroners and smelling bad.

At Brunswick Street, I re-dressed myself from top to toe at an op shop, then threw my stinking rags in a rubbish bin. But there was still my hair. I walked into the hairdressing salon where Kyle's favourite cutter Jeremy worked, but he was off today.

'Doesn't matter,' I told the woman who was on duty. 'I just want it all shaved off. A number one, please.'

She clutched at where her heart was supposed to be and shrieked, 'No! Don't shave it!' And she started telling me what I should do with it and how it would look best, when all I wanted was to be rid of the damn hindrance.

'Look,' I told her, 'it stinks. Just get rid of it!'

She had the electric clippers on and buzzing when the big glass doors flew open. I heard Kyle's voice screech, 'Stop! Don't do it! This girl has just come back from Sydney. Obviously she's in no state to make a decision!'

I looked around at Kyle, framed like a goddess in the hair salon doorway, and at last felt relief. She was the closest thing to home I had now. We chatted about Sydney while I had my hair washed and cut, and then we braved the heat and Brunswick Street.

'How d'you know I'd be here?' I said as a host of trams crashed by.

Kyle shrugged. 'Where else would you go? There's only Brunswick Street.'

We watched the trams and the traffic for a while. Kyle was waiting for me to talk. I tried to tell her about Marcie, but I couldn't get the words out.

'Listen,' she said, 'I dunno what's been going on, but Shane's locked himself in the bathroom back there. Now, I'm all for kooky behaviour, but it's a small house, you know?'

I shrugged. 'S'pose.'

She took hold of my arm in such a way that it seemed like I was helping her.

'Good,' she said, hailing us a cab.

The bathroom was completely white. Tiles, paint, bright white. White bath, white fittings, white shower curtain. In the middle of the white floor was a brown ceramic bowl with a vegetable mixture inside. Beside it was a brown ceramic bong. I felt like getting down on my hands and knees to praise it.

'Looks like you're becoming a social creature,' I told Shane as he locked the door behind me. Eyes rolling, blood-shot and spun halfway to the moons of Saturn, I could tell he wasn't going to be any fun.

'You took ages,' he lamented, as if he actually *had* been waiting for me. The bong was an extension of his hand. I smoked it in and told him about the weird things I'd been doing. Hash lightened my mind and brought back all the colours and smells. As I talked I noticed my voice had gone down a couple of octaves. Slower too. I said I really needed a bath. I needed to get rid of the smell.

Ten minutes later, I was reclining in a warm bubble bath, sweating from the day's heat. Sweating out Marcie.

Shane came in with some clean clothes, and for a moment I contemplated being bashful. I wasn't in the habit of socialising from the bathtub. But being bashful necessitated trivialising, and I wasn't in a trivial mood. So I said nothing and he said nothing, and we sat and smoked so much hash that the black grout between the white tiles lost its distinction.

'She fell apart when they moved her,' I told him finally.

He had his back to me, and his long hair was half submerged in the dissipating bubbles. When he shook his head in disbelief, the hair stirred the water like a lazy fibrous spatula. I picked up one long dreadlocked clump and squeezed out the water.

Kyle was bashing on the door. 'I don't know what's going on in there,' she called out in her queeny voice, probably to amuse the people in the kitchen, 'but I'm dying to go to the toilet.' Shane turned his head to me, and his hair slipped out of my hand. He hadn't even realised.

'Let her in.' I didn't state it as an order. He didn't take it as a command. Nothing that had gone down between us mattered any more. Not in the face of Marcie.

The look on Kyle's face when she walked in almost distracted me. Yeah, I was in the bath with no clothes on, and Shane was looking glassy-eyed. She misread the situation with glee. I had no energy to respond to the insinuating looks.

'Guys,' she said with forced reason in her voice, 'I really have to go.' Shane locked the door behind her, saying nothing. Glaring impatiently, she realised that there was no way that either of us were budging. She shrugged, then went about her business. I waited until she had finished on the toilet then told her about Marcie.

They'd been best friends once upon a time, Kyle and Marcie. Raging out at all the pubs and clubs. That was until I came along, and Marcie discovered the mind-numbing potential of barbiturates. Kyle looked like she'd been shot. Drained and frozen. She was silent. I told her I had polaroids. Kyle was a brave woman: she wanted to see them. Shane got them from my bag and handed them to her. She looked like she'd been shot again. Handing them back to Shane, she looked at me gravely. She didn't say anything. There was nothing to say. For Kyle, it was a first.

It was fine until I ventured from the bathroom. There smack in the middle of the kitchen was Big Danny Herlihy. It was a small kitchen. He was a big guy. I couldn't miss him. We hadn't seen each other for a while. Not since Brendan died. It brought back feelings I thought I had a handle on. The wave of horror.

Suddenly, I was out on the street and arguing with Shane, and we were just as crazy as each other, so there was no hope. Not with Brendan hovering so close. I told Shane I loved Brendan because he was so generous. Shane told me he hated Brendan for turning me against him when something really positive was happening.

I turned and looked him close in the eye, so far gone

that I probably looked together. 'Something positive?' I said slowly, although I knew full well he meant our Ash Wednesday fuck(s). He knew that I knew, and it totally killed him. I realised instantly that he was very sentimental, in love with some vision of me, and would probably never talk to me again.

My house was a cesspool of red tape and blue uniforms.

DO NOT CROSS!

A bullcop with his shirtsleeves rolled up in the early evening blustery heat retrieved DS Moon from inside. Behind sunglasses, in someone else's clothes, sporting a new hairstyle, I could be whoever I wanted to be. This evening I was a far cry from the stoic earlier model. I masked my sleep-deprived temporary insanity with vulnerability.

'I just had to drop by and pick up a few things,' I told him, my voice wavering. 'I can't stay here. Not yet.'

Moon nodded and said, 'I understand. And if you feel the need to talk about it, there are people who can help.'

I rolled my eyes. Luckily, Moon presumed I was looking at the action on the staircase. 'What's there to talk about?' I said. 'She knew the risk she was taking.'

Moon nodded. 'Well, when you're ready, come in and make that statement.'

I smiled to myself as I stepped past him, thinking to myself, Like hell I will.

My room was as I'd left it. Nothing had changed since New Year's Eve, except there were a few more butts in the ashtray. I collected the dole cheques that Kyle had stashed in the Bad Seeds album cover (always wondered what happened to the record), and then stood in the middle of the cavernous room in cynical contemplation. My material possessions. Twenty three years of experience, all of it pulled from back lanes. Fourth hand, fifth hand, Thrift and Opportunity.

From above my desk, a picture of Hunter S Thompson and Oscar Acosta at Caesar's Palace. Miniature hash pipe. Brendan's Foghorn Leghorn comic. A photo of me and my long-haired hippie brother. Some condoms.

When it came down to it, I didn't need much.

Gertrude Street was warm and dry and smelly. Armed with the feeling that I would never walk it this way again, and an overstuffed handbag, I gave lip to people who even glanced at me. I was hyped-up, at a dangerous loose end. Maybe I could go back to Shane's house. I was going to have to do something about that guy.

Damn it, Brunswick Street. Damn it!

It could have all been so different. He likes me: I like him. I could be at home now, in bed with him.

Brunswick Street. Red light.

If I wasn't such a stupid coward.

CHAPTER SIXTEEN

Fearless

At the corner of Gertrude and Brunswick, my attention was drawn to a passing tram. Arms were flailing from one of the windows as it rattled along, and above the cacophany I heard my name being called.

'Caitlin! Caitlin, you harlot!'

It was Sly.

He was riding the routes with his new boyfriend, a tram conductor named David. They met in Paris, when David was on holiday and Sly was a patient of the Pasteur Institute. Rich parents sent him there to see if the virus gnawing at his immune system could be destroyed. The virus was still alive, and so was Sly, but his folks couldn't take the risk. He was disowned, along with the shame of the gay plague, which caused him a certain amount of grief, he admitted, but not for long. David was his family now.

As the tram turned into Collins Street, and began to rattle down the hill through what was ambitiously known as Little Paris, he said, 'I was in Paris when Brendan went. Sure was a terrible waste of human life.' It was with a laugh in his voice, as was everything Sly said. I smiled in defiance of the day and said, 'A culpable waste.' Sly looked out of the window thoughtfully and said, 'Mmmm. He had such a cute butt.'

The tram slid further down the hill, and closed in on the City Square. A seventies concrete monster, good only for skateboards and roller skates, both of which were banned. It was a warm summer evening, with a city crowd to match.

'Oh, look,' said Sly flippantly, 'There's Bindy.'

Bindy was a girl we used to know. She played trumpet in a jazz band and dealt good hash. Out on the footpath, the wind was blowing and her long stringy blonde hair was dancing around as if she was being electrocuted. She looked pale and there were big shadows where her cheeks used to be. I was trying to tell myself that *perhaps* she had a chronic iron deficiency, instead of the obvious, when I noticed her stop a man in the street, her hand on his arm. She appeared to know him. When I took a look at his face, when long hair wasn't blowing over it, I realised I did too.

My stomach knew it before my brain did. It felt like it was going to fall out on the wooden floor of the tram. The hair and clothes were all different, but the eyes were the same. The eyes of a Botticelli angel.

'Fuck!' I said under my breath at least ten times, like some demented cuckoo clock stuck on the hour. I knew it was Cal. I knew it. The tram slid me away, across Swanston Street: I yelled at David to stop the tram and he did, just beyond the traffic lights. I thanked him, said goodbye to Sly and then jumped out. Two cars almost hit me. I wasn't thinking about earthly things. I tore to the intersection and looked around, crossing the road again and again in the hope I hadn't been hallucinating. In the end I sat down on the Town Hall steps, feverish and dejected. Even my hallucinations were deserting me.

I scored Big Danny Herlihy as taxi driver on the cross-town run back to Carlton. Danny was radiating amphetamines, almost frothing at the mouth. I let him talk and took in all the lights, framing as they did elusive images of Marcie and Shane and Brendan and Cal. Most of them made me sick. That, and the caffeine. I was tired, jittery and spun out. It was only 10.15.

'Have a busy night, Danny,' I said cheerfully as he dropped me off on Rathdowne Street. It was dead quiet. I had no idea what day it was, but it seemed too quiet, even for a Sunday.

'I bloody hope so,' he mumbled half to himself. 'This pure speed'll be the death of me.'

Six weeks ago I would have begged him for some. Now that thought made me feel sick. I waved goodbye, and he was gone in a blur down the dead bright street. Across the road, the commission flats were quiet. Everyone tucked up in bed. No one here but us ghosts.

CHAPTER SEVENTEEN

The risk of destroying everything

The front door was open. The air smelt like incense. The lights were on.

'Anybody home?'

It was a tentative call, not in my own voice. Shane appeared in the dining-room doorway. When he saw me, he went really low, as if I was a hassle he couldn't get rid of. I'd planned my words carefully, but they all went out of my head when I saw his face in the dim light of the lava lamp. Multiple hues of orange over the deep dark crevices of his eyes. I tried to sound together, but it all came out garbled.

'I've just been wandering around. The things that have been happening – ' Fucked it up already, I knew it. 'Shit!'

Nothing sounded right. He stood frozen in the doorway, with that almost demonic look on his face. Like there was nothing I could do to shift it. He went to fold his arms, and some paper in one of his hands fell to the floor as if he'd forgotten all about it. I looked at it. He looked at it. Then he sighed, picked it up and held it out to me. Still the alien voice, devoid of life, 'This came today. I don't know if you want to read it or not.'

I stepped closer and took hold of the paper and he released it immediately, as if I might contaminate him. The letterhead said 'District Coroner's Court'. I could just make out the type. 'Report into the death of Brendan Kennelly'.

The paper was orange and glowing in the subdued light. I knew it was going to burn all the way down. Just like Shane's eyes. What was he doing with the report anyway? What was his interest? Why was I always looking for a change of subject?

'Can I be honest with you?'

Eyes mean and angry, he looked like he wanted to spit. If I was going to salvage the situation, I had to do it quick. Explanations got me nowhere: I couldn't explain feelings.

'Whenever I have sex,' I said, my voice shaky through nerves, 'I imagine it's you.'

I was sure I was going to die on the spot.

He was stunned. He believed me.

And then I did it. I told someone about Cal, for the first time. Only my brother knew the story: he didn't know the hurt. Reliving it made me sick to the very DNA, but I kept talking. About the inability to trust, how casual sex was preferable to involvement, how it was easier to evade than be honest: how I thought he might understand. How seeing Marcie on the floor today made me see the beauty of life and the potential in him.

He started off listening from his post by the living-room doorway. Gradually he moved closer, and ended up holding my hand when I finished. From there, it was inevitable, and I was glad. Sex with him seemed to be my only possibility of salvation. He stroked the back of my hand and said, 'I love you.' I didn't reply: he didn't seem to mind. And when we went into his room, where it was hot and quiet, I didn't think about Brendan or Cal or anyone else. No faces flashed before me: no guilt or rage or hurt. I was too nervous. It was like the first time. Only better.

I watched Shane while he slept, with the spears of dread stabbing me all over, and decided I must love him. Either that, or I had an intestinal problem. I determined never to let him or myself get hurt again.

At 3 AM Roman burst into the room and started yelling, 'Wake up, Brophy, you lazy son of a bitch – ' I dived under the sheet, praying he hadn't seen me in the darkness.

Next to me, Shane stirred and sleepily mumbled, 'Piss off'. There was a short silence, when I thought Roman might have taken the advice, until an earthquake shook the bed and I realised that in his drunken stupor he was jumping on it.

'It was great! I saw all the old crowd! Went to Todd's place, where they threw a little party for me – I've got some of this beautiful crystalline speed for you – caught a glimpse of Her Highness Caitlin Princess of Angst getting into Danny

Herlihy's cab. I really think you'd be better off forgetting about her, Bro, she's more neurotic than you are – '

'Quit jumping on my FUCKING BED!' Shane mumbled, feeling for me in the darkness under the sheet. As his hand came in contact with my bare shoulder, there was an almighty upheaval, and the jumping recommenced on the floor.

'Oh, come on, Bro,' Roman was yelling as the hand slid across my arm to my breast, 'we've got some speed, some weed, some tequila. Come and have some fun.'

Shane pulled me close to him and told Roman, 'I don't DO fun.' And then he kissed me, and I guess Roman realised someone else was there in the bed with him, because he quit the theatrics and closed the door behind him. Muffled noise came through the weatherboard walls from the lounge room. We sighed in relief, and shared a demure laugh. Then Shane let go of me and lit a candle.

'At the risk of destroying everything,' he said in a low, tentative voice, 'there's something we really should talk about.'

I put my arm around his stomach. It was in knots. Brendan. I knew he meant Brendan. Memories of all the pain came up. I fought to keep them at bay.

'Two things, really.' He was lying on his back, looking at the ceiling. 'Firstly, I was completely overwhelmed from the moment you answered the door that day when I was looking for Brendan. I just couldn't get you out of my head.

And maybe what happened on Ash Wednesday was just casual sex to you, but I knew exactly what I was doing. And it was worth it.'

I felt sick and strange in a pleasurable way. I'd always seen Ash Wednesday as my initiation. Some good honest dirty fun. I had completely misread the signs. I remembered him saying, 'That's what I love about you.' But I thought it was just a line. Now, in the hot dark room, it seemed like yesterday, as if this was a continuation. As if the last twelve months hadn't happened.

'That's the first thing.'

His tone told me the second thing wouldn't feel quite so good.

He turned and looked at me. 'In the coroners report' – my whole body went into icy paralysis – 'something's not right. The toxicity levels are incredibly high. Like' – he was speaking gently, slowly, unsurely – 'I know he OD'd, but it was a really massive overdose.'

I tried to find my voice. 'How massive?'

He reached to a bedside table and produced another group of papers. The police report: Dekkar's and Kyle's statements.

'They tested the remains in the foil.' He flicked through the pages then found the pathology report, indicating small type with his finger.

I shook my head, to indicate I couldn't see it in the candlelight.

He closed the pages, closed his eyes and said, 'Ninety-five per cent pure.'

My mind started swirling, entering a cloud of shock. I said, 'What?'

He looked at me as if to say, You heard.

My mind sailed back to New Year's Eve. To Dekkar frantically trying to revive Brendan. Not understanding why he wasn't breathing. Pure dope. That would explain it. Ninety-five per cent. It was lethal. He didn't have a chance.

'I had some,' I mumbled to myself. 'It was strong, but not that strong.' I shuddered. What was he doing with almost pure dope? More to the point – I turned back to Shane – 'What are you doing with all these reports?'

He closed his eyes again. 'We were close once.'

It was the saddest and most confused moment of the day. Right when I thought all the ghosts were buried, they'd come out to haunt me.

CHAPTER EIGHTEEN

Straightforward

At 9 AM, I fronted at Fitzroy police station and gave my statement to the young policewoman who'd been first on the scene. I was straightforward, describing fairly truthfully what had gone on, minus Shane's appearance. I told her yeah, Marcie was a junkie, because there was no point hiding that. Half of the Melbourne cops knew that already. It took about an hour. When it was finished, I put on a weak emotional front and asked if they knew yet what had happened to Marcie. I was told that because of the state of her body, it would take some time to determine. But what, I pressed, as if I was going to get distraught, did she OD? Was she bashed? Raped? Did she suffer?

The policewoman cupped her hands and told me she doubted that Marcie suffered. The traces of dope in the syringe were very pure. In all likelihood, it would have been instant. Marcie probably had no idea how strong it was. I shook my head and covered my face, and she went to get me a cup of tea, assuming I was upset.

I was more than upset. I was boiling.

The mind works quickly in anger. Walking along Johnston Street, a scenario played out before me which was so incredible it must be true. I remembered when Brendan came home with the story about getting busted after scoring, and his suspicions about Marcie turning grass. A couple of weeks later he gets a hot shot. A couple of weeks after that, so does Marcie. It was simple. It was hideous.

By Rathdowne Street, I was shaking. It was still morning, already very hot. I ran the last block to exhaust some of the nervous energy then bashed on the front door of Shane's house. I knew he would be there, waiting for me. He was good at waiting.

Roman answered the door, pupils still wildly dilated. 'Oh, so you decided to show your face.'

I pushed him aside and told him in a low voice, 'I was here all night, and I've got the sore cunt to prove it!'

Aghast at my crudity and desperately trying to top it, he smiled and said, 'Well, that explains it, then.'

'What?'

'The place is still a mess. I always said Shane only went on his manic cleaning binges out of sexual frustration.'

'Can it, Roman!' I stepped into the lounge-room and scanned the speedy faces until I found Kyle's. I'd already decided she was the only person I could go to with this. Taking her by the arm with the lure of gossip, I dragged her into Shane's room. He was as I had left him, sprawled naked and sound asleep across the bed. I said to Kyle, 'You sit there,' positioned her on a red rocking chair, then ran my hand through Shane's hair. A difficult endeavour because of the dreadlocks. He woke up with a start when my fingers got caught somewhere at the back, then smiled with his eyes. Confident I had what I needed, I told Kyle everything. I tried to be gentle, but there is no easy way of telling someone that the boy she'd known since childhood had been, in all likelihood, murdered.

She was quiet for a long time, locked in her own nightmare, which was compounded by speed and drink and lack of sleep. Shadows of conspiracy hung behind her exquisitely painted eyes.

'For God's sake,' she said, gesturing towards Shane, 'cover that naked man. I can't think with naked men around.'

It was good to laugh. I pulled a sheet over Shane and he buried his face in his hands.

Kyle nodded when it was done. 'Are the cops going to do anything?'

I shrugged. I hesitated. Then I said, 'I think it's more to the point to ask are we going to do anything?'

She wiped a stray tear from the corner of her eye, and said in a low voice, 'If it's true, if someone deliberately OD'd Brendan – ' Her voice was full of hate. She didn't have to say any more.

'We get to them before the police do.'

Shane buried his face beneath his forearms. I hated

putting him through this, when all he wanted to do was love me. That's why Kyle was there. I turned to her, unsure how she was going to react. Most of the things we talked about doing never got done. The things that did get done usually involved men, drugs or hair dressing. Now, her eyes were burning as red as a hell hound. Unabashed at what I was suggesting – hostile retaliation – she wanted to get out there and do it.

'You always used to hassle me,' I said, trying to change the subject and calm her down, 'cos I was so lazy when it came to scoring. I only ever got stuff delivered to the house: when Al went out of the business, I always got you or Brendan to score for me. I never asked where the stuff came from, because that made me think what might be in it.'

From his muffled position over the other side of the bed, Shane let out some kind of exasperated laugh.

'That's right,' Kyle said, as much to Shane as to me, 'I've never seen anyone so squeamish about taking drugs. Ever! Except Duane. He faints at the sight of a needle.' Shane's face came out from hiding, and it was smiling.

'I wasn't that squeamish,' I said in my own defence, in the hope that by ridiculing myself, I would make them both laugh, 'I just have very bad veins, a weak stomach, and I bruise easily. And I want to vomit every time I see a soup spoon.'

They got it like only junk fiends would. Kyle was grinning widely. I zoned in and said, 'Where did the dope from

Marcie's suss liaison with the cops come from? And the stuff from New Year's Eve?'

Her mouth dropped and she said, 'Let me think,' before she rose and took a new position, standing at the window staring at the closed curtains. She was calculating. She was reliable. But she needed time. So I turned to Shane and we fooled around for a couple of minutes. That part was simple.

'I'm not sure about the night the cops ripped off the gear,' Kyle said from her stance at the curtain. 'But New Year's Eve, it was definitely John the Score. That's what they call him round the brothels, anyway.'

The name meant nothing to me. 'I don't know what he looks like.'

Kyle gave a laugh and said, 'That's the easy part. He does two-hourly runs down Fitzroy Street.' She looked at her watch. 'Yep, he's due in twenty minutes.'

I turned to Shane, hoping I wouldn't get an adverse reaction. Deep down he was vulnerable. I had to tread carefully if I wanted to maintain what I had.

'I have to go,' I told him, and he nodded. After Kyle had gone to get herself organised, Shane drew serpents up my arms with his index finger and told me he didn't want to curb my style. That's why he wanted me to be careful. I said that it was strictly fact-finding: Kyle had to sleep off the speed before she could make any kind of intelligent decision. I didn't ask him to help, and he didn't offer.

We were in the bathroom, getting ready to go out. The air was thick as a Sydney skinhead.

Kyle was checking her nails and twisting her mouth, literally choosing her words. 'Something I have to say to you Cait.'

It sounded ominous.

'I was glad when you went up to Sydney. I thought you were driving us all mad. But as soon as you left, it all got so dull, so dead boring, the only thing to do was take drugs, and that wasn't much fun either. Now you're back, and there are things happening again. Pretty horrible things on the whole, but it's better than a slow death.'

I was taken aback.

'So what,' I said, flicking a lazy arm in the air, 'you'd rather have decomposing bodies and suspect deaths than a tranquil life?'

'Personally, I'd rather have a good-looking man and a bottle of Jim Beam.' A smile crept onto her lips. I knew she was going to say something outrageous. 'Any good talent at the cop shop?'

I screamed, 'Kyle! That's disgusting! You wouldn't!'

She laughed, pleased to have shocked me. 'I dunno, it's getting pretty desperate. Sometimes I think it would be really nice to have a relationship. Other times I think, Nah, the only men worth having seem to carry so much excess baggage that a little affair would be like a full mountain trek.'

I nodded thoughtfully – not very thoughtfully in truth, just one or two random peregrinations – and said, 'In many ways men are more trouble than their worth. What do you say we go and get a dildo and become lesbians?'

Kyle didn't flinch. She really could take anything. She applied a bright red slash to her lips and said, 'How can you say such things when you've got that guy in there eating out of the palm of your hand? I mean, how did you do it?' I don't think she really wanted to know what I couldn't explain.

'I don't know. I think he needs his head read.' And I rolled my eyes like it meant something.

We lapsed into a bemused silence, making like we were lightly entertained when in truth we were both thinking strange and foreign thoughts.

You know the pain/that's in my heart/it just shows I'm not very smart –

Tape player full blast, Black Flag doing Louie Louie, we were cruising it in style along St Kilda Road in Roman's Zephyr. Just borrowing it for a few minutes, we said. He didn't know neither of us could drive.

Who needs love/when you got a gun/who needs love/to have any fun?

Full on lead breaks, we were dancing in our seats. It was turning us psychotic. We were going to get this sorted out, regardless of the cost. Brendan was our blood brother. He was running through our veins by the time the song had finished and we hit Fitzroy Street.

'Right, so let's check this arsehole out!'

Kyle was getting more aggressive by the minute. There was a tough brawler in there just itching to get out. She crawled the car down the drag and sorted through the early morning trade with a hawk eye and a sharp tongue. 'Hah, look what she's wearing. Look at that, on the nod on the street, pa-THET-ic. Look, there's Billy the anarchist eating a meat pie!'

I wound down my window and yelled, 'Shame, Billy, Shame!' and we laughed like hoons until she pointed and in a low yell said, 'There he is – there.'

I followed the invisible line from her index finger. A small crowd were coming out of one of the restaurants. When it cleared, and I saw who she was pointing to, I was shocked and sick and overjoyed.

Cal.

'Okay,' I said with a loud clap, rubbing my hands together, 'he's mine!'

Of course, being daytime we were both wearing sunglasses, so I couldn't tell what her eyes were doing. But the tight-set smile on her face gave me some indication. She was a woman after my own heart.

The clock said 10.50 PM. The streetlight streamed through a gap in the curtains. I was naked, sore and with complete recollection of the day preceding this night. Driving round with Kyle, going home to Shane's, going shopping at the Vic Markets, turning Shane's room upside down to find some Rohypnols to put Roman out of his babbling misery. Just hanging around, doing crosswords and kinky sex. I remembered it all. Just the way I liked to wake up.

My clothes were in the vicinity of the bed. I dressed, applied make-up, then sat down and had a long think. I thought about Cal: about how much I thought I loved him. How amazing it felt the day he said he liked me too. How entirely decimated I was when he betrayed me. How he left that feeling in my gut: how I would never trust anyone the way I trusted him. Strange, but in the years since it had happened, revenge never entered my mind. I was always taught to go with the flow. I blocked the memory down a damp passage of my mind, along with the other near-death experiences and traumas. Now Cal had come back. If he'd stayed in my memory, I could ignore him. But he was back. And he'd dealt Brendan a very pure deal. I could not ignore that.

Kyle came in, refreshed and looking divine in a blue velvet party dress. Just inside the doorway, she discovered Shane's records and created a fracas.

I'm waiting for my man/twenty-six dollars in my hand –

Dancing around the room to where I was sitting on the bed, she sang along in a deliberately raucous rant until she bent down and said into my ear, 'They're all in the kitchen.'

Potential eavesdroppers. And I thought she was getting off on Velvet Underground when she was stoned. She pulled me up and got me to dance with her.

'While you were fucking the Iceman, I was out mixing it. Guess who I ran into at the Prince of Wales?' She didn't wait for the courtesy query. 'John the Score, that's who.'

My head buzzed with pleasure. Blood surged in time to the disjointed music.

'He offered me a taste for a fuck, later tonight. He'll be all alone: he'll be expecting me. You know what you said earlier – '

He's never early/he's always late –

I smiled. 'I want to get him.'

She smiled. 'Right.'

First thing you learn/is that you always got to wait –

'What if it's not him? What if it's got nothing to do with him?'

We danced for a moment, and I thought about it. Not for very long. 'I still want to get him.'

She scratched her nose, swung her hair from one shoulder to another and assumed her serious dancing expression. Dodging pieces of furniture and land mines, she flailed her way across the room, singing, ' "I'm waiting for my man." ' Turning when she reached the door, she yelled above the noise, 'Okay, let's go do some business, girl.'

Shane was in a little studio room at the back of the house working on some sort of computer program. I could tell by his eyes he was stoned. He looked very natural and relaxed.

'I'm going out with Kyle for a while,' I told him. The plastic shopping bag in my hand rustled. A piece of rope was hanging out. Eyes fixed on it, he scratched his chin and in a low and calm voice said, 'Let me drive you. I'll worry myself insane otherwise. I don't want to know anything: just let me drive you.'

I didn't know what to do. Torn between wanting to keep him right out of this and wanting to keep him happy. I was not used to moral dilemmas. In the end I decided he was just too beautiful to leave at home. Within five minutes we were in the car. Kyle and I sat in the back, lapping up the chauffeur, singing along to the tape: '"She's like heroin to me, she's like heroin to me, she cannot miss a vein – "'

CHAPTER NINETEEN

The Big Rush

It was right on midnight when we pulled into Burnett Street. It was big and wide and reasonably quiet. Shane pulled the Zephyr to the side halfway down the street. The block of flats where Cal lived was thirty metres away and in plain view. Kyle stared at the plastic bag in her hands for several moments.

'Second thoughts?' I asked her.

She shook her head. And shook her head again, then looked up, eyes ready for action. 'So when it's all set, I'll flick the light twice in that front room.' She pointed to a window, glowing red.

'Okay,' I said, and I took her hand.

'Piece of cake,' she muttered, extracting herself from the car and cutting a stunning shadow along the street in the white vinyl coat and long black wig.

I was talking to Shane about all kinds of things. Politics, art, writing, religion. The more we talked, the more I realised I had much to learn about him. I'd always assumed that because he was a semi-regular junkie, all his energy went into that. Not so. His father being head honcho of a drug company meant he never had to go out looking for drugs. Instead, he had some kind of part-time consultancy with the Health Department's media strategy think tank. I was amazed that something like that existed. Then I saw the light flicker twice in the third floor flat up the street. My stomach dropped to the bottom of the car. Shane leant around from the front seat and kissed me so deeply and intently that it felt like sex. He could do things with his tongue that didn't bear thinking about.

'John the Score,' he said quietly as I slid across to get out of the back seat. 'It's this Cal guy, yeah?' I wondered for a second how he'd sussed it out. Then I decided not to. Some things are better left as mystery. I nodded. He said, 'Take care – and control.' Leaving him was agony.

The staircase was solid concrete. The bricks of the building were a deep, dark red. They were radiating heat from the last couple of days. Up two flights and I came to the doorway labelled '6'. I took a deep breath and said, 'You're in control.'

Kyle answered the door looking completely cool. As I slipped on my gloves, she lead me through a lounge-room done out in pseudo-Mexican design, around a corner, to a bedroom. I'd tried to brace myself so I didn't fall apart, but nothing could have prepared me for what was in the bedroom.

A huge double bed. Heavy red velvet curtains. Red silk sheets. A naked man lying face-up, his arms and legs tied to the four posts of the bed. Blindfolded, gagged. I turned to Kyle and we burst into simultaneous cackles of laughter.

The body on the bed picked up my laugh and started squirming. Kyle laughed as she said, 'It's okay, John, I've got a special thrill for you tonight. I've brought a friend along.' We moved towards the bed.

I whispered, 'Are you sure he's secured?' and she feigned annoyance, saying, 'This ain't the first time, honey.' The banter kept my nerves at bay, until I went straight up and lifted the blindfold.

His eyes were dull and set, but they were still that bright green. The boyish charm was gone, but he was a striking looking man. The bastard. I smiled at him.

'Hello, Cal. Remember me?'

The look in his eyes denoted a negative.

I smiled again. 'Caitlin. You owe me seven and a half pounds.'

He was spinning away. It was too much for him. Poor dear. I went to the kitchen and collected the biggest knife I could find. Some kind of butcher's knife, gleaming and lethal. As I took the nine steps back to the bedroom, I knew that this sort of thing could easily get out of hand. Nailing people's heads to coffee tables and all that. Cal was sprawled out, completely helpless. I had a knife in my hand, brim full of malice. I could have done a lot of things.

Then I thought about Shane, waiting in the car. It was enough. I took a deep breath, then went back to the bed. Eye contact. He hated me and he was terrified.

I ran the smooth side of the knife down his disappointingly scrawny torso then held the sharp side under his balls.

'Where's your stash, big boy?'

His mouth made murmuring sounds. Like he had something to say now that it was an apparent robbery. Kyle lifted the tape over his mouth slowly, saying 'No loud noises, or I'll let her loose on her initial suggestion for you.'

We grinned at each other as the tape peeled off slowly. He spat and stared at me almost plaintively. Yeah, he still had his looks, but he was losing them fast.

Masterful.

'Your stash, Cal.'

My heart was going crazy. I hoped he would submit, having a hankering for submission, judging by his position. The plaintive look continued until he said, 'In the kitchen. Milo tin.'

Kyle jumped to go and get it. I put the tape and blindfold back on. I didn't want to see him any longer than I had to. I wished I had a cigarette.

'Hardly a stash,' Kyle said as she came back into the room, holding a half dozen foils in her hand. 'There's only three grams here.'

I looked at the foils, looked at Cal, then back at Kyle

and said, 'It should be enough. Three grams'll be just fine. You go and sit in the lounge if you want.'

She sniffed, cool and smacked out, and said, 'What are you gonna do?' She had no idea.

'Payback,' I said with a smile. 'Leave it to me.'

She was wearing knee-high boots, suspenders and some kind of leather bra. Head shaking, she said no, she was staying put. She was the most beautiful assistant I could wish for.

Mixing the foils into the water in the soup spoon, I was too deep in thought to notice if I was squeamish. When it was as dissolved as it was ever going to get, I started looking for a filter. Then I decided, What the fuck. It didn't matter anyway. I sucked the liquid straight up into the syringe. It filled up the entire dropper, seemingly alive. For a second I thought I was going to be sick. But I controlled it. I headed back to the bedroom.

Kyle was sitting on a chair in the corner of the room. I went to the bed, took some rope and applied a tourniquet to Cal's arm. His skin was white. It was obvious he was not a physical man. The insides of his elbows were brown, almost like callouses. When his arm was ready, I lifted the blindfold.

'I'm going to kill you now,' I told him with a smile in my voice. He started thrusting about. I pinned down his arm with my knees. It was there, right before me. I had the chance to rethink my plan. It was sound.

I shot him up.

He froze. In the split second before the smack or what-ever he was peddling reached his heart, a trace of his boyish charm shone through. The Botticelli eyes smiled. His true love had him. The Big Rush.

'Shit!' Kyle said, jumping up from her position in the corner. If she meant to stop me, it was too late. Cal's eyes closed slowly, dragged off by the rush.

'Oh, my God,' she went on, 'I don't believe this.'

I tossed the fit next to him on the bed and washed my hands of the whole stinking business.

'What did you expect me to do?' I said, gathering her clothes. 'Give him a medal?'

Kyle shook her head, watching Cal intently. I searched around the place for her shoes, wondering if Cal was hover-ing above his body. Just in case, I turned to the ceiling and fingered an 'up yours'.

'Shit!' Kyle cried out again, this time in real fright. I jumped along the hallway to the bedroom, almost drop-ping her shoes.

'What?' I said.

'Look!'

Cal's eyes were open. He wasn't dead. The bastard. He must have *some* habit. His eyes were glazed, taking in the ceiling with a smile.

'What are we gonna do?'

I felt a sudden wave of nausea. It was as if, down at the

morgue, they'd moved Marcie, and a gust of her stench had reached me. I couldn't go through it again. Not any of it.

'Give him a medal,' I told Kyle, helping to put her clothes on.

She said a few things, like, 'Shouldn't we untie him?' and, 'Shouldn't we close the front door?'

I didn't answer, and I didn't look back.

CHAPTER TWENTY

Nature strip

The grass on the nature strip was dried out and shaven. The bitumen welts either side radiated heat. The baby wattle made a brave attempt at providing shade.

Shane came walking along from the direction of the shops. My stomach still felt sick when I saw him. But a nice kind of sick. He flopped down on the dead grass beside me.

'I just heard,' he said slowly, 'your mate got done last night. Cal. Supplying. He's in Pentridge.'

'Wacko.'

I was smiling, but it was no victory. Brendan and Marcie were gone forever. Try as I might to blame Cal, or drugs, or the capitalist system, they were still gone. There was no meaning in that. I turned to Shane.

'Do you think there's any point to this existence?'

The sun was beginning to set over the terraces across the road. I watched it with calm resignation.

'Nope.'

Shane's eyes were smiling. Far from mastering a spontaneous grin, at least he was learning. Tracing an invisible serpent along my arm with his finger, he added, 'But there are things that make it enjoyable. You know: Films. Sex. Drugs. Greek food. The alchemical transformation of housework.'

He rustled the plastic bag he'd been carrying and I looked inside. Implements of cleaning. Rubber gloves, fluids and disinfectant. He really did have a thing about order. I rolled closer to him on the grass and put my head in his lap.

'It really is over, isn't it?'

He slipped on his sunglasses and reclined, trying to make the shade go further.

'Off the space shuttle, Cait. It's only the beginning.'

A mild wind whipped up, cooling us down at last and rustling the plastic bag of cleaning gear. A couple of scourers escaped from the plastic bag and danced along the naked nature strip.

I watched them go and wished them luck.